BISON
BOOKS

FLYOVER FICTION

Series editor:

Ron Hansen

Another Burning Kingdom

ROBERT VIVIAN

University of Nebraska Press   Lincoln & London

Library of Congress
Cataloging-in-Publication Data
Vivian, Robert, 1967–
Another burning
kingdom / Robert Vivian.
p. cm. — (Flyover fiction)
(Tall grass trilogy)
ISBN 978-0-8032-1107-0
(pbk.: alk. paper)
1. Brothers — Fiction.
2. Nebraska — Fiction.
3. Psychological fiction.
I. Title.
PS3572.I875A84 2011
813'.54 — dc22
2010029426

Set in Minion and
VAG Rounded by Bob Reitz.

This book is for my father, David James
and my brothers, Bill and Bart

Now I know that the Lord will help
  his anointed;
He will answer him from his holy
  heaven
With mighty victories by his right
  hand.
Some boast of chariots, and some of
  horses;
  but we boast of the name of the
  Lord our God.
They will collapse and fall;
  but we shall rise and stand
  upright

PSALMS, 20:6–8

Contents

Acknowledgments

I wish to thank here and forever the following bright lights: Brian Evenson, Aaron Gwyn, and Philip Graham, for their keen reading and feedback that helped me to find my way through this book and others.

I wish to thank my first and foremost reader, my wife, Tina, who is always there to listen and to respond, wherever the prose takes me.

I wish to thank Ann Baker, for her painstaking copyediting though many books together.

I wish to thank Ladette Randolph, for believing in the vision of this trilogy.

Most of all, I wish to thank Kristen Elias Rowley and Heather Lundine, who have provided a home for this writer in a world of homelessness. My debt to you both is ineffable, my gratitude a life-long prayer and joyful reminder.

Another Burning Kingdom

REDUX AND RECOIL

Jackson

The ghosts of Lem's horses are screaming again. They sound like shrieking women falling from the sky. They circle round the house half a story high with their manes tracing gossamer wings in the moonlight. I've gotten to know them so good they're like someone breathing right down on top of me. But only I have eyes bright enough to see them. Some of them look like bent, moaning trees before they rise up again to take on the stars staring down on all of creation. I never meant to kill Lem's horses. But once you start in on something you have to finish the job, and nobody would say any different if they were up front about it. But hardly anybody the fuck ever is.

Lem knows but he won't say.

He's always not saying the most important things to me. I have a list of the speeches he won't tell me that goes on a mile long in some tunnels in the ground. I'm his alpha and omega, and a few hundred other things besides. That's how it is between us. Lem's horses won't leave me alone, and I accept full responsibility for it: all neighing commences the coming of the kingdom and you better get that straight in your head. One of the stallions has teeth the size of picture windows looking out on eternity. I've never heard of a man-eating horse before but maybe there are some you can corral if you know where to find them.

Vengeance is mine, sayeth the Lord.

And he wasn't bullshitting when he said it.

Lem is the best brother I could ever have but he thinks he's failed me. I feel his sadness like a magnetic force field that doesn't get weaker with the miles. He never liked what I had to say about America, but it pours out of me in panoramic visions that light up the sky in nuclear pastels and radioactive snow that twinkles before it hits the ground. He says I'm crazy, and maybe I am. I know Lissa believes it. But I've seen the tears well up in his eyes when he said it. I love him so much it's like an ache I can't get rid of.

He's my brother and best friend and like a father to me past our real father, who wasn't worth a shit and tried to drown me once. But sometimes that means Lem has to flip sides and be an enemy, too. If it was all just one way we'd be more fucked than we already are. Lem's older than me by a good seven years but it sometimes feels more like centuries. He sees no good use for violence, but I see its untapped potential everywhere around: you could throw a stone far out into the night in any direction and whatever it hit would be fit for a streak of destruction now and then. And that's exactly where this nation is headed and where it needs to go, right into the mouth of the lion with burning flames for a mane.

But me and Lem always were two different halves of the same good book.

That's why I had to kill his horses that time, hard though it was for me, and harder for him. Someone had to do it, but not all of them died right away. Horse blood isn't like other blood, there's more of a shimmer to it, like sheet metal.

I tried to explain it to Lem but I couldn't keep the sobs from choking me up like a net full of butterflies. I have a hard time saying

4

the most essential things unless the spirit's in me, and then there's nothing I can't say. I can reveal the world in a drove of speech. God gives it to me to say in brief bouts of clarity and then I'm shining with judgment in my eyes. I can't help it either way. Lem knows that better than anybody, but he can't bring himself to admit it. Because if he did everything he ever believed in would crumble down around him, which it will anyway. Only he can't see it. There's a plan that set all of this in motion and I'm just a small but necessary part of it. Lem isn't imbued like me; he's as fine and decent a man as there is. He's weak when it comes to drinking and Lissa but I don't hold that against him. God loves him like an acorn in his hand. It's true I'll shoot anyone that comes up to the house now, but not out of spite: I'm just doing what I have to do to make the Lord's plan a go.

Lem's horses don't worry me so much. Without their bodies they can't trample the ground. Their hooves are made of air so they can flock and scream all they want, their thunder has been washed away by a force greater than any stampeding herd.

How did I go about mowing them down? How did I shoot them one by one fourteen strong so they laid there like dark bleeding hills bringing swarms of flies from miles away? I'll get to that before it's over. I promise. I'll explain it when the spirit comes upon me — when I can say it in words with a branding iron for my tongue. Until then I have to wait, locked and loaded. I've been up two nights straight and am working on a third. Adrenalin has been replaced by the flow of glory in my veins. My final vigil has commenced. I don't expect to live twenty-four hours beyond it. God bless my last cigarette: its glow is sacred in His eyes. I'm waiting for Lem. I got ahold of him and he said he's coming home to try talk to me one more time. It's not like the other times and I told him that. I've always known it would end like this. The other burning kingdom's almost here.

Who dreamed me into existence?

Who dreamed you?

Jackson, I say, God made you this way for a reason — and with this reason comes a thousand sons and daughters, not through the propagation of your seed but the transmission of your *deeds* that must be carried out. That's all it is, all it ever could be. All I have to do is wait a little longer, but it's a waiting charged with holiness. It doesn't hardly matter how long you live, only that you're going to get reborn.

Rebirth has come. Everything's been leading up to it. Lem's horses have become whirlwinds, but they'll settle down to dust eventually and go on back to being anthills. They'll go back to where they came from, hauling their screams. I almost like them for company, even though they're outside and I'm in here, smoking my last pack of Pall Malls like a burning heap of rubble, panning the dark lip of the horizon that's about to say something. If only I had ears enough to hear it.

Lem

I'm driving out in the middle of the night to come see you, leaving everything behind, including Lissa and the kids who don't see me much anymore — not since I moved out awhile ago. I'm a better brother than I ever was a father, and that ain't sayin' much. Lissa and me have been trying to make it work, but I've been away so long it's like we're always starting over from square one and getting off on the wrong foot somehow. Now I'm coming out to see you, driving twenty hours straight with just three stops for gas, staring at bathroom walls of scraped Fuck Yous.

She didn't like it when I left, but she didn't like it when I stayed.

That's how things are.

I started smoking again — but I always do when I know I'm gonna see you, and when we're together I couldn't quit if I tried. Some things just fall together in crowds. Sometimes it seems the only thing that makes any sense is when I haul my ass out to Western Nebraska to make sure you haven't gone and blown yourself all to hell, taking some poor innocent sucker along with you. So at least I gotta give you credit for that, for giving me a clear sense of purpose once in a while. If you weren't my brother none of this would be an issue: I'd let them lock you up and throw away the key, let you blow yourself up into a thousand pieces. Wouldn't make a shit of difference to me. But I know I'm fooling myself, which is a double disgrace. It's not hardly half true and we both know it, know it so well that you never needed to play that card.

Neither did I.

Neither did anyone, not even God.

Because it always just was, always just is.

But Jackson, I can't keep coming out there every time you get into trouble or start talking your blue streak of mayhem. Sooner or later someone's gonna catch a whiff of your so-called visions for a brand new America rising out of the ashes and then they're going to take you away for sure, with no tick-tock left for come-uppance. Blowing up barns and getting thrown in jail for being drunk is one thing, but what you're talking about now is so off the charts I don't even know what to say. We gotta set down and hash this thing out once and for all. I can't do this anymore. You need help. Time is running out for both of us. I'm almost fifty-two and you're forty-five. What do we have to show for it? An alienated wife and two kids I hardly know for me, traveling around the country doing part-time scouting work for the Angels, and you living out in that sorry shack by yourself, getting more and more isolated and paranoid, passing the days dreaming up God knows what. I can't even bear to think about it. But if I fail with Lissa, I don't want it to have anything to do with you. It's got to be on my own shoulders. I can't let her blame you, and that goes for me, too. That way if it ends it'll be sad but honest and clean, which is the most I can hope for now.

I can't even fucking say for sure anymore.

I'm grasping at straws, Jackson, I got nothing left in the tank. I'm coming up empty. You don't even have to be a brother or an uncle any longer — not that you ever could be the latter, what with Lissa afraid of what you might pull if you were around the kids long enough. I can't say I blame her. But if you could somehow figure out a way to live a quiet, normal life out there in Arrowhead, that would be a good and positive thing, the most hopeful thing I can think of, almost a slice of heaven for the relief it would give to everyone who knows you. Because it's important to have your head on straight, Jackson. And it's even more important not to hurt anyone, starting with yourself. That's all I want for you — and yes, for me, too, goddammit. I admit it's selfish, but not all of it is. Some of it's concern for you — beyond that it's just plain concern of the most basic humanity variety, nothing more complicated than that. So don't go and start dreaming up hidden motives or telling me I don't know anything about it. America has nothing to do with it. Neither does God or Mama or how he left us, or what he did right before he took off for good.

Because you're getting worse, Jackson.

You're saying shit I never even heard you so much as hint at before. I didn't tell Lissa half of it, didn't want to make things worse than they already are. And I don't want to go into it, what you did to those horses two years ago. That's over and done with. I must be as crazy as you for not making you face the music for what you did, which almost anyone else would have done in that situation, brother or not. But what you're talking about now, putting innocent people at risk has got nothin' to do with your radical ideas — it's beyond troubling, it's an altogether different magnitude of fucked-up.

This is still a beautiful country, Jackson, the shining hope of the entire free world. Why can't you see that? Nothing's gonna change that hopeful fact, certainly not a homegrown terrorist from Arrowhead, Nebraska. I can't fucking believe it's come to this. People are flocking from all over the world just to live here, thousands of

Mexicans pouring in over the border each day. I see it everyday in my own backyard. Why are they coming here? Why? Because it's better than where they come from, pure and simple. America's not as lost as you think it is, or as dead to its ideals. It's just the same huge, sprawling place it always was, where anything can still happen, including somebody plotting and scheming like you. You don't need to save America from itself—because it doesn't need saving.

It never did and it never will.

But it's not too late even now, and we both gotta believe that. We can turn this thing around and get you the help you need. No more bullshit from either one of us. Enough is enough. You need to hear this straight up from me, and I'm gonna tell it to you this way when I get there. I'm the last link you have to reality in this world. That's how out of touch you've become. I can't keep bailing you out every time you get into trouble or threaten to do something. My influence is wearing thin, if I ever had any. It's practically as see-through as one of Mama's old tablecloths by now. Jesus, I thought you were collecting those guns because you admired them, like some kind of hobby or sport. I didn't know you were stockpiling the sons-of-bitches for the end of the world. You're starting to scare people, Jackson, including me.

So here I go, four hours out of Glendale at four a.m., pushing eighty-five and trying to get some kind of head start, listening to all-night talk shows and police scanners, hoping not to hear any breaking news about you. I figure I have a day and a half, tops. That's how things stand. Trooper pulls me over, wants to know where I'm going in such a hurry, there's no way I could even begin to explain it to him or anyone else. *Well, sir, it's like this: I've got this brother in western Nebraska who's threatening to blow up the state capitol building in Lincoln — you know, the one with the nineteen-foot Sower on top. I'm the only one who can get through to him. That's why I'm speeding. Because if I don't get there soon he might just follow through with it.* If you just had some kind of regular human contact things might be different. You might have a reason to be more engaged and less full of whatever it is that you've been pumping into your veins. I'm always dreaming up scenarios for you, thinking of how things could be this way or that way, which is definitely a waste of my time. I can't help it. It's the worst habit I ever acquired, dreaming up how things could have been different for you.

Now it's come down to this.

I'm the only one who can put a framework around what happened to you, Jackson, and try to make sense of it. I know that now. I guess I always have. You've never been a burden to me, no matter what anyone says. You're my brother. Fuck, what else is there to say? Lissa always said you were the most important relationship in my life, and it used to piss me off when she said it. I fought her tooth and nail on it, never wanted to hear it. She didn't even say it to be spiteful, she just said it because it was true. She was right, and I realize that now.

But my priorities have changed. They *had* to change. Now so do yours. I got my own last chance with her and the kids to salvage what I can, and it's looking pretty grim already. It's probably too late for me and Lissa, but I can at least be there for Sam and Scottie. At least I can try. So it's the last chance for all of us all the way around. That's what I'm gonna ask of you, to just try. Because something's different this time. I can feel it in the air between us, like some kind of static electricity. It's not just one way anymore. I've got questions for you, Jackson, I've got things I wanna ask *you* about. And for once I expect some straight goddamn answers.

Why did you think those horses were mine, Jackson?

What put that idea into your head?

They just wandered in from somewhere in eastern Colorado, a freakish equine event. They didn't belong to anyone, only to the land they wandered in on. You lured them in and then you slaughtered them one by one. I don't even know how you did it. When I found you and started cleaning up the mess, you just kept jabbering on and on that they belonged to me.

I keep trying to pinpoint the exact moment that leads up to a man finding himself speeding through the middle of the night across half the western U.S. in order to try to stop his brother from carrying out a terrorist threat, something he can't tell anyone about because if he even breathed so much as a word about it, it would be all over, done, finished: you'd never be a free man again, sick or well. But if I have to turn you in myself I will. I think you know that, Jackson. Maybe that's why you called me like you did, to help you find a way from not following through with it. So I'm laying it all on the line, and maybe even right now risking people's lives, people who go off to work each morning, drop their kids off at school, pay their bills, watch football on Saturdays, dream their own dreams. But I just can't believe you're serious about what you're saying. I don't want to believe it.

So we'll sit down and have a long talk about it, light up like a couple of old-time smoke hounds, which is exactly what we've become. Stay up all night and the next if we need to, however long it takes to get some things out in the open and clear between us. We don't have to rush a thing. I need to look you in the eye, to see your overall condition. Because the last time I saw you, brother, wasn't exactly inspiring. You looked like you had dwindled down to the size of a scarecrow. I still don't know where the hell you got all those burns around your neck, but it looked like someone had been dotting you with lit cigarettes or some other damn thing. And that was a year and a half ago, the last time I laid eyes on you.

You call me up out of nowhere from a pay phone a night and a half ago, going on about blueprints and air ducts, people's names I never heard of, serial numbers, enough to scare the shit out of anyone. I heard you say the words but it was like someone else was listening. I couldn't make heads or tails of what was coming out of your mouth. I didn't want to. Lissa didn't even ask this time, and I didn't bother to tell her: she knew it was bad. I didn't promise her this would be the last time. I'm done making promises. But she let me go, no discussion, no argument, maybe because it was so late and she's been working so hard lately. So that's all it took. Maybe that's progress right there, the fatigue that wears you down so you can't even question things anymore. We even used to joke about you sometimes, called it the Jackson Factor. Used to be able to almost laugh about it.

But all of that's over. I'm listening to music in the middle of the night like I never heard it before, hearing it with ears hollowed out with dread. I'm afraid of what I might hear, Jackson, some far-off explosion, some mushroom cloud lifting high up into the sky, a newscast breaking in. I keep telling myself that nothing has happened yet, it could all be in your mind. That's the one hope I keep coming back to, the one that keeps me going. So just sit tight till I get there, it won't be long now. Don't go and do something stupid. I'm asking you this as a favor, the last one I'll ever ask you. I'm practically begging you, Jackson. Please, brother, just wait till I get there. We'll sit down and talk, I won't rush to any conclusions. Your secrets are safe with me. I couldn't tell them to anybody else even if I wanted to, because there's no words to use that anyone would understand, including me.

Lissa

I keep dreaming of horses. I have for a couple of years now. In the dream they're running in from a long ways off, out of some cloud or mist, with their thundering hoofs even though they're always quiet, almost like they're flying. The wind isn't rushing through their manes, the wind *is* their manes, along with the sun and the stars and the moon and all the rest of it. Then they turn into smoke that rises high into the sky, and then it's over.

Lem never had to tell me about what Jackson did because I already knew. Jackson told me, the one time it was just the two of us, the night I thought he was going to try to do something to me. Lem still has no idea about that night or that I know what Jackson did. If he did it would tear him up even worse than he already is and might make him start drinking again. But Jackson and I have always had some kind of understanding between us, one that didn't have to use many words. He believed those horses belonged to Lem, he gave Lem the power of their possession in his mind. In a strange way that I don't even understand myself, maybe Jackson was right: maybe they were Lem's horses after all. So I don't dislike Jackson, I'm not even afraid of him anymore. I just think he's lost his mind. I don't begrudge him his visions or his ideas, I just don't want the people I love anywhere near him, especially Scottie and Sam.

Lem is trying to make up for lost time, but it's too late. I can't bring myself to tell him yet, but I think he already knows, or suspects it anyway. So that's another one of my secrets now, another one I can't share with him. You go all these years as open as can be, and then suddenly you discover you have a secret you can't share that seems to be pressing down on you a little more with every passing day.

I've been having my one and only affair with a man ten years younger than I am. Not like Lem, who had a string of one-nighters out on the road and ended up telling me about them one by one when he called home weepy and drunk at three a.m. It's amazing to me now how hysterical I used to get, all that yelling and issuing him ultimatums — now I'd probably just sigh and shake my head. I have no intention of ending it anytime soon, and I know how selfish that sounds. His name is Ray and he's awfully good to me, so good I don't know what I'd do without him right now. I don't love him the way I used to love Lem, not even close — you only have energy for that kind of love once in a lifetime — but I no longer need that as a requirement. It's not even an issue. I'm not having this affair to get back at Lem; the whole idea of revenge just sounds ridiculous to me anymore. I didn't go out of my way looking for Ray, he just kept coming around the store, talking and being friendly. Sometimes that's all it takes. One day I just let him into my life, and he waltzed right in, filling it up with light and laughter.

He couldn't be more different than Lem — he's not haunted by a tortured past, for one thing, and he doesn't care if he makes a fool of himself. He'd do anything to make me laugh, and I mean anything, and for some reason that's very precious to me, almost as precious as Scottie and Sam. Just the other day he got down on his knees and sang to me in an Italian restaurant with all these people around: I must have turned five shades of red, but I have to admit, it moved me. It's not even the gesture so much as the *willingness* to do it, to put his male ego on the line. That's new in my experience.

Lem would never admit it, but he's too much of a loner to sustain a relationship, especially marriage. The only exception is Jackson, no matter what kind of trouble he's gotten himself into. It's true, he's not been a very good husband, but I've never seen a better brother. Besides that, Lem can't stay in one place longer than a year or two before he has to up and leave and go somewhere else. What I've come to realize is, it's not even an excuse anymore, just something he has to do. I no longer blame him for this, but it's no way to stay married and raise kids. I see him like I never did before because I was too busy feeling sorry for myself and worrying about what was going to happen next.

But not anymore, no, not ever again.

At some point in a marriage the man you used to love so much just becomes a man, and you see him with all his faults and all his virtues too. That's how I see Lem now. He's always been haunted by what happened to Jackson, not to mention the way his own dreams fell apart, including me. I was there when it was happening, or as close as I could be. Lem would call me in the middle of the night from the road, and those conversations were some of the best we ever had. He'd *talk* to me like he couldn't when we were in the same room or in the same bed, and maybe it was the distance between us that made it possible, that gave him the space to open up. I'm not threatened by that space anymore, and have come to even understand it in a way. We used to joke that we'd have a great marriage if we could just keep a few hundred miles between us with free long distance calls.

But I fell in love with Lemmuel Purchase the first time I saw him, and the funny part is, it was just his back I saw standing there at a party in Pasadena with Fleetwood Mac playing in the background. How can you fall in love with someone's back? But I did, and it was a strong, upright back, as straight as could be, how he still carries himself today even after all those surgeries on his back and knee. I almost didn't want him to turn around, not because I was afraid I wouldn't like his face — he's still one of the best-looking men I've ever seen — but because there was something about watching his back that endeared me to him right away, and much, much more than that.

I didn't waste any time. I went right up to him, tapped him on the shoulder, and we eloped four months later. I couldn't care less that he was a professional baseball player, I'd never even been to a ball game before I met him. I knew baseball was America's pastime and all that, but it bored me to tears. Nine guys standing around in brightly colored uniforms scratching themselves, talking into their gloves, making signals like the Three Stooges. I thought it was almost funny. But after I got to know Lem I saw how much baseball meant to him — and once I started to watch him play I could tell that he was good. I mean really good. Before long I realized something else about Lem and baseball: it wasn't just a game to him, it was more like he was playing for his life. So no matter what I thought of it, I could see that it was one of the most important things in the world to him because it's who and what he was.

Then one night in Oklahoma City during the night game of a double-header he was trying to steal second and he slid into the bag all wrong. The team doctor said it was the worst injury he'd ever seen. I was back here in Glendale with Scottie, who was about three at the time, and Lem's once-promising career was unofficially over. He was never the same again — not the same player, not the same husband, not even the same man. Like a lot of young men he thought he was indestructible, and when he tore his knee the air just went out of him. He tried to come back after five different surgeries, even tried to switch positions and become a pitcher, but it was too late. It seems that's been the theme running throughout our lives together, *Too late, Too late,* like some kind of background music. Then he started to drink and fool around and I was pregnant with Sam before he moved out the first time.

On good days we called that difficult time Strike One. On bad days we knew it was the beginning of the end. But the truth was, it was already pretty much over. So we had seven, maybe eight good years, and once the kids came and the injuries and the drinking, well, you kinda lose track pretty fast that way, jumping straight over your middle years into early middle-age, where I felt fairly content despite everything, until Ray did a two-step into my life. You'd be surprised how easy it is to have an affair, at least I was. It's almost like learning how to breathe again because it *is* breathing a new kind of air when you can't find any oxygen in your own marriage, which isn't even a marriage so much anymore, except on paper. I tried to tell Lem about it a couple of times in my own way, but he was so clueless I couldn't follow through with it. So that makes me a chicken on top of everything else. I keep telling myself the time isn't right, but of course it will never be right. And that's almost funny, too, because for all the times Lem slept with other women, it's like he never really cheated on me. One, two nights, and it was over. He always came back to me, contrite and sober, vowing not to do it again. And he meant it every time.

Lem will always be coming back to me, even when he hasn't gone anywhere.

That's partly why he's such a sad man.

He's haunted by his own life and what it could have been, haunted by Jackson, his mother, the father he never knew, his entire past growing up in that tiny town. I only went out to Arrowhead with him twice, and I couldn't wait to get out of there. It's not even the town so much as the way the sky presses down on you from all directions with no relief in sight, all that blue and streaks of clouds that somehow take a part of you with them every time they go. I kept thinking the town and everything in it was about to float off into the atmosphere, vanish altogether because of too much exposure. It's not that you feel tiny in that part of the country, it's more like you're just a speck of dust waiting to be blown to the ends of the earth. I don't know how people live there year after year, to be honest. But maybe it's different if it's all you've ever known. It might even be beautiful, just a stone's throw away from the moon and the stars.

Lem's told me I don't know how many times that he's never going back but he always does, every time Jackson's teetering on the edge. But even that's not the whole story, because there's something about Jackson Purchase that a person needs to know more than anything else, no matter what he does or talks about doing, no matter what his delusions are: he really is touched in a way, not like anyone else you're ever likely to meet. There's a kind of purity about him, too, even integrity: I don't think he's capable of lying. I think maybe something happened to him that not even Lem knows anything about, something so bad and tragic that it warped him into the person he is. In another time and place maybe he could have used his almost-otherworldly gifts in a less self-destructive way, like a prophet or a shaman. I truly believe that. But then I have to remind myself, sometimes harshly, that Jackson hasn't turned out that way, that, for all of his derangement, he's made some choices for which he must be held accountable, choices that no one, not even Lem, can save him from.

Strangely enough, the one thing I've always been able to somehow count on over the years is Lem taking off because Jackson's in trouble, each time a little more bizarre and disturbing than the last. I don't even want to know what it's about anymore, because all it does is fill me with dread. And not just for what happens to Lem either, but for me, for the kids, for anyone who happens to be around Jackson when he has one of his meltdowns. After Jackson told me what he did to those horses that one night I slowly backed away from him and out of his life for good, where I hope to stay. Lem doesn't have to know what he told me, but he knows I no longer want to see Jackson. I think he's afraid to hear the real reason anyway. So he goes out to try to help him, but nothing is ever solved or resolved, as far as I can tell. Jackson's never any closer to getting serious help, let alone a cure. For the moment, at least, the situation has been defused and something bad has been averted.

This last time, I don't know, it feels different somehow.

So here I am at the ripe age of forty-six, full of secrets and betrayals, which seem to be getting deeper with every passing day. But I don't feel guilt anymore, I refuse to feel it, and I've learned how to do that, how to refuse to feel things that can't change anything. I'm glad I gave up guilt. Glad I'm not going back to it again. So at least I've done a one-eighty in that department. Now I feel my life opening up again with just a sliver of daylight, and that daylight has a lot to do with Ray. I don't know how long it will last, but that doesn't bother me. It's enough to know we'll go out to have Chinese tomorrow night, then see a movie. The kids are grown up now. They have been for years. Lem doesn't understand that because he wasn't around, but the people he's suddenly so keen on getting to know aren't the same ones he left all those years ago. We went through the crying and the anger together, we went through all the stages of grief and not understanding why he is the way he is. Now we know and it doesn't have the power much to move us, which is a breathtaking thing to admit.

When people leave, you learn how to manage without them, and whether they come back or not just isn't as important anymore because part of you has already left with the one who keeps leaving you. So that's how it is. Lem thinks by staying around the way he is now that he can somehow patch up the holes, but what the poor guy doesn't understand is that even the holes aren't there anymore: he's chasing after ghosts, in the kids, in me, in Jackson, and maybe, even especially, in himself. The kids love him to death but they're so used to living without him that they can't just drop everything and invite him back into their lives. Neither can I. The only one who can is Jackson. Or maybe it's Lem who can't live without Jackson. Maybe that. He keeps saying he's gonna get Jackson some real help, but he never follows through on it.

I think he almost needs Jackson to be sick, to have Jackson depend on him somehow, so he has somebody in the world he's accountable to. I don't hold it against either one of them. Lem practically raised Jackson when their dad left. He was more of a father to his brother than he ever was to his own children. But it's a combustible closeness, one that could go up in flames any second. That's the reason why I worry about him going out there. Jackson's getting so sick he might try to hurt Lem in his screwed-up dream world.

When Ray touches me, he touches me all over. There's no part of me that's off limits. He goes so far down it's like he passes through the other side of my skin in a moan, and I'm right there with him to meet him on the other side. I feel new as a woman again, more desirable than I've ever been. And it's not just because he's so much younger than I am and he can't keep his hands off me. He understands how I'm made and he wants to know how every part works. There's a trembling curiosity to his touch and all the rest of him, and I'm able to give of myself in a way I couldn't with Lem, because whenever Lem and I made love I knew he'd be gone soon. At the beginning I even thought it was a little romantic, but that wore off in a hurry. Lem needs a highway in front of him, stretching all the way to the horizon, needs days and nights of driving between destinations, whether it's for baseball or for Jackson or for his own demons that he's wrestling with listening to sports radio. That's probably where he feels most at home, or maybe most himself. He doesn't have to explain it anymore, let alone defend it: the people who care about him know it better than he does.

He called me from his apartment late last night to tell me he was driving out to Arrowhead to see Jackson. He didn't give me many details and I didn't ask. We have a shorthand when it comes to Jackson: the fewer words, the better. Still, it feels different this time. Lem's voice wasn't the same. He sounded shaken, almost spooked. Jackson can have that effect on you. I know that as well as anyone. Lem's been sober for several months now, the longest span since he started going to AA. But when he comes back this time I'm going to tell him everything — this time I know I will.

I'm going to tell him about Ray. Because I can't let him start to believe we're going to try to make it work. It's over. But first he's going to see Jackson. I wonder how many times I've had that particular thought, *First he's going to see Jackson.* But this is one last time and then it will be over. I won't have to pretend he's my husband, and he won't be making plans for us that can't come true. What Jackson will have to say about that, I don't know, but he probably knows already: he'll probably tell Lem before I do. So in the meantime, for this one last time, I will wait for him like I always have before. Then I won't have to wait for him ever again as his wife. We'll both be free from this pathetic joke of a marriage, and maybe then some good will come out of it, because it has to, because for once it will be honest and true, the way things are and the way they have to be.

Not even Jackson will be able to destroy that.

Jackson

Now the first one is coming back to me, breaking away from the others, just like I knew he would: he's such a sweet sonofabitch he can't hardly help it, circling back like a high-up cirrus cloud coming in for a better look on the nothingness it presides over, the same nothingness that blew breath into me and gave me my song of soulful destruction. He's so beautiful and graceful with his long sleek shanks made of radioactive fallout, I want to sweep him up in the sigh of a whirlwind. I loved him the most and that's why I had to start with him. Even now he understands what I had to do and is the only one that doesn't want to trample me into rabbit bones and bird brains, to stomp out my staring mouth and kick out my eyes.

I call him Hiroshima, or Hiro for short, because of what he represents: nuclear winds sweeping along at 300 miles per. I can tell he wants to eat something out of my hand, but I don't have anything to give him, not even a Cheerio. All I have is a bucketful of ashes. If he comes back in a week or so I can give him my body and my life, but till then he'll have to go away forlorn, which makes me wanna weep every time. With a high-stepper like him all you can do is put the first one in his lung, then kneel down at the altar of his shining throat and slit it open deep and wide.

Lem could understand, if he wanted to.

He could infer the necessity of sacrifice and wear it like a crown. That's all I ever wanted for him, to be the man he was handpicked to be — not a prophet but a prince, the shining hope of this fucked-up land. I wanted Lem to be more than my hero, I wanted him to be a god. We had to pay together and separately for that calamitous idolatry. The Lord gave him to me to worship in order for it all to come crashing down, and it will before long. False worship must be annihilated so that genuine worship can again take place, even if it's only a single pinwheel spinning in the sun. What I must carry out can't be accomplished any other way: that's the meaning of God's word and all the poetry in the world, along with the radical agents of change that must have their day.

Because America has betrayed itself.

America has whored itself out to the lowest bidder.

And America must pay for that now, beginning in Lincoln. I've studied and pondered it from every angle and premise, I've prayed to the Lord of distance and the rising sun, *Please, God, take this grievous cup from my lips*, but it was not to be, He deigned to show me the truth and will not suffer half-hearted measures by way of response and reckoning. That means some things will have to burn, and I too must go down in flames.

Or did you think that we would all somehow be spared?

After Lem they'll come for me, and I will face them and show them what I know until it's stamped and seared in their memories forever. The end can't be stayed much longer, but they can only know it by burning. The white horse knows this in a way the other horses don't, which is why he keeps coming back to me, breaking away from the rest of them. His eyes are made of pure sky, his nostrils wide open and flaring into the void.

Now he's coming up to the window in a patch of visible breath, wanting to breathe his ghost life into me. Some intimacy is so tender no sheet could ever whisper it. The white horse is just a few beads of dew now, a tablecloth of condensation touching my fevered brow: his vapor's singing in the voice of a breeze. If the other horses knew me this way we'd all be breaths together and they wouldn't keep racing around the house before the sun goes down, seeking to kick up the dust of the place where they were killed. Only the white horse knows to approach on legs of perspiring grass, where the light comes in carrying handfuls of rainbows.

In my mind I see Lem driving. He's forever driving to me. His knuckles are wrapped around the steering wheel, the passing light of oncoming headlights scan across his forehead cragged with sorrow and the memories of pine tar: the crows have mapped out their ancient winters around his eyes and the cracked lines therein. He's smoking and road weary, swaying slightly to the hypnotic speed of his trajectory over the barren contours of the highway that hold him like a lost son, talking to me in dream speech prepared by his perpetual bewilderment. *Jackson, you need help. No more fooling now. I'm your brother and I love you. You can't keep doing these things or saying you're gonna do them. They'll take you away and lock you up for sure.* I know that, Lem, I know it all too well. I always have. But such things were never up to me alone. All I did was submit and try to live inside the truth.

Lem doesn't want the truth, he wants to leg out a triple like he used to — then he wants Lissa back. He wants what he had so abundantly and briefly that he didn't even know he had it until all of it was gone. That's the meaning of his life that he still doesn't know, which haunts him every night at three a.m. when he goes to take another aching piss on the second floor of his apartment that overlooks a cactus garden the size of a baby's coffin. He's a man who doesn't know himself, or Lissa, or his children either, let alone me. So he must learn his lesson at the hands of someone who loves him enough to kill him. He thinks he's coming to save me, to get me help, but the truth is he's coming to be liberated from falsehood once and for all, which is the best and only gift I have left to give him, the only true gift I ever had to give. I will liberate him from a legion of lies in a blinding flash of revelation, and then he can go to his one true home that can't be found anywhere on this earth. Inside his waking visions he carries the dreams of an entire nation, all its pennants, races, and Fourth of July porches with sparklers going off, the hope of a new day, a new season, new crops, the first cup of coffee in diners all across America.

He's the land I love so much it has to rise up out of the ashes in order to be reborn.

I see his broken spirit in a thousand telltale gestures, some of them so small and heartbreaking they emit a low-pitched moan nobody can hear but me and a few dolphins out near the eastern seaboard. Lem has become a tragic figure but he doesn't know it yet. All his disappointments and sorrows are merely a prelude to what I'll have to give to him like a kiss. And this is why I've never begrudged the long desert of my vassal-hood: because I'm no more than an instrument, the smallest one in the world.

What is a nation that has forgotten the need for sacrifice, starting with one's bone-lonely self in the unflinching act of self-immolation? Moths know this better than most U.S. citizens. Everywhere I look I see the handiwork of cowards and whores on billboards all the way to Denver, in 1-800 numbers, golden arches, satellite TVs, Humvees that deserve to be compacted into battered suitcases of nil: I see what this nation has become and I vomit up a putrid bile of disgust that stretches from New York all the way to Oregon. But all of that's about to change: these rife defilements can't be sustained anymore. Lem could tell you that, if he was here. He could confirm the worst of the best and the best of the worst, the solar

26

flare-ups inside my tear-stained eyelids. He can't deny the truth when we're together. All he can do is shake his head and sigh. That's what makes him so dear and precious to me, what makes him the beloved of the one and risen Lord. He just can't keep going the way he has, is all. His end is my end *and* the end of this country. He needs someone to shoot him out of his own mouth and life, out of his own worn-out dreams, and the only one that can do that, the only loving and deranged enough to do that one hard radiant and terrible thing, is me.

Lem

I try not to think back any more than I have to, but it seems the past is always catching up with me, especially when I'm out here with all this open road knowing I'm gonna see you in a day or two. I guess driving and memory just go hand in hand. But I'm tempted to keep going once I hit I-80, drive right by Arrowhead all the way through Iowa on into Chicago. Maybe stop and see a buddy of mine, go out like old times in Wrigleyville, minus the booze. I think I can manage that. Eight months is pretty good for an old sot like me, not a single sip of anything stronger than O'Doul's. Tell the truth, I don't hardly mind the nonalcoholic stuff they serve these days: the taste is there all right, even if the kick isn't.

Even Lissa is impressed by my restraint.

You wouldn't miss me that much, Jackson. You really wouldn't. It's like you stare right through me to whatever you think you see anyway, oceans of falling-away space. We were never like any other brothers that I know of: too much of that notorious Purchase chemical imbalance running inside our veins. The sonofabitch is probably still alive somewhere, living in some mobile home park where the snowbirds go, taking advantage of some poor little old woman. I wouldn't put it past the old bastard. But for my part I hope he's dead, and I mean dead-dead, with termites for a mouth. I used to have to tell you everything about him, trying to fill in all the blanks, all his little idiosyncrasies and what-not, the way he entered a room. It's like you were born brand new after he tried to kill you, thinking he was killing me, the way the slate of your mind was wiped clean by the lack of oxygen to your brain.

Hell, Jackson, you know there's never any end to that discussion — so you don't have to get so caught up and concerned with the so-called state of the union or where this country is headed and all the dire straits you keep talking about. You wouldn't have to be so obsessed with things no person can change. We could talk about how he broke my arm that time, how he used to dance with Mama in the kitchen on the rare good days, all the bad things and the all the pathetic ones, too. He was a mean, nasty drunk if there ever was one, whereas I've always just been a quiet drunk — and you never had to touch the stuff because you had other things to worry about, like coming back from the dead. But you've always had a leg up on me, for saving my life down by the tank when he came looking for me practically hovering in the air after drinking all that grain alcohol.

I don't know how many times I have to relive it, but I keep going back there. You're supposed to be my little brother. Hell, you *are* my little brother, and you go and do a foolish thing like that, something I can't possibly ever live up to. No one could, not even Jesus himself. Even if I would have made it into the Hall of Fame nothing would ever change the fact that you were willing to die for me — and that you did die for me for twenty minutes the day he threw you into that icy water to drown. He thought you were me, Jackson, he was coming for *me*, and when he got sober he didn't even remember what he did or tried to do: he couldn't believe it himself when they told him about it behind bars, before he broke out and disappeared for good.

So what in the hell can I do with any of that?

I know you don't remember it, so I have to remember for both of us. Maybe that's the real reason why I drop everything and drive out to see you, to remind you of what you don't remember and what I can't forget. I don't begrudge the rehashing of it, even though it sounds like I bitch about it all the time. I just have a feeling that this time it might be better if I kept going, though you and me both know I won't follow through on it. I just got to get certain things off my chest sometimes, even if it's to the roof of this Buick, to convince myself there are different possibilities other than you talking about things no one can understand.

Lissa thinks I still feel guilty about you saving my life even after all these years, but I've tried to tell her it's not just that. It's more the responsibility and principal of the thing. I want people to know what really happened to you so they can try to understand where you're coming from, the cruel twist of fate that made you what you are. You used to call me a hero, but what I never could convince you of is that you're the real hero — you're the one who should have married a beautiful woman like Lissa, should have had all that green pasture ahead of him, not me.

Here I've gone and fallen back into the same old goddamned rut, one so worn out and familiar I know every crack and curve along the way. You'd think I would have gotten tired of it by now, but it's just another part of what we share. This time I'm not gonna deal with any hypotheticals — no *if* you get help or *if* you talk to someone. I'm gonna take care of them the minute I'm sure you haven't gone and hurt yourself or someone else, when I can persuade you that the sky's not falling in. I know I've got my work cut out for me, but there's nothing new in that. Sometimes when I look into your eyes it's like they're hauling you out of the water all over, like you're seeing things that aren't even there. I remember how they brought you up to the surface, how the first thing I saw was your open eyes ten feet under, slowly coming up surrounded by a column of air bubbles from the divers, how you looked like you were staring at something no one had ever seen.

The doctors said it was a miracle you made it at all. What they didn't know is that a part of you didn't. I can't even say what's happened is water under the bridge because the water's always been there between us, and always will be — the water that you delivered me from and the water that created a new Jackson after they dragged the dead one out of it. Because I remember a different Jackson, an odd little kid who liked to draw with wristbands on, who wouldn't hurt a flea. The only thing that didn't change is your hardcore stubbornness. That hasn't changed a bit.

There's something about this late-night driving that makes me see a few things in a whole new light, things I can't put into words once I get to where I'm going, though it always feels like I'm heading back to Arrowhead. I could end up in the middle of the Congo somewhere and I'd still somehow, some way be driving back to you. This is as much a mystery to me as it is to anyone else — you, Lissa, or God himself, who you seem to have gotten to know so well lately.

I didn't dive down into that cold water after you, I just stood there hiding and waiting for him to leave. Those were the longest seconds of my life. He was so out of it he could hardly stand up, weaving back and forth on some invisible stem, staring into the water where he threw you in. He told you to "Swim, goddammit," thinking it was me. Then when you didn't come up he staggered back to the truck and drove off. And that was pretty much the end of him in our lives. But I never ran so fast, Jackson, not even when I was stealing bases and turning singles into doubles. My own breath couldn't keep up with me. Once they hauled you out of there and managed to get your heart pumping again I somehow knew it would always be like this, going back to that day for the rest of my life.

31

Maybe the best part of you died and stayed on the other side. You've got to admit that possibility. I've tried to see what you saw the way you tell it to me, but it's outside of my grasp altogether. You were always the one with the vivid imagination, not me. I can't see it like you do. I guess I never will. But if you love Jesus so much then you can't mean all the things you've been talking about lately, not to mention what you did to those horses that weren't even mine to begin with.

I thought I was seeing a mirage that day. If you weren't so isolated, so far out in the country someone would have seen them for sure and locked you away for good. How you went about executing them one by one, telling me it was for my sake, for my glory, you called it, I thought I had lost my mind myself. I don't know why you thought they had anything to do with me. We were never around horses growing up. You were sitting there in the center of them, covered in horse blood, babbling nonsense: the kid who went into that icy water for my sake never would have conceived of such a thing, let alone carried it out. Cruelty to animals or anything else just wasn't in him.

Maybe this last and final time you can explain it to me and I'll understand — not what you did, but why you did it. You kept saying over and over, *I killed them for you, Lem,* saying it was all for me. But Jackson, goddammit, I don't know what the hell to do with that, I don't know why you thought you had to do something so heinous like that in the first place. It's outside every known category altogether. Maybe I'm anguished and haunted, just like Lissa says. But who wouldn't be after something like that and all the rest of it?

What's the fucking alternative, anyway?

No one's ever been able to give me one. Not to care? Not to say these things happened and that they mattered? To let them all go? To let you go? To say you saved my life and just leave it at that?

To ignore you when you call? To pretend driving out here doesn't matter? That you're not my sick brother who gave his life to me? That I'm not an alcoholic who used to be addicted to painkillers? That I haven't failed and fucked up as a husband and a father? That I didn't realize my dream of making it to the show? That I didn't drink myself out of every coaching job I ever had?

All these things have to make sense somehow. I refuse to believe they don't. I'm not holding out any hope that you're gonna get any better: I know you're not. All I want now is for you to know that I did the best I could for you, that I listened when no one else would. I owe you that at least — and a helluva lot more. I always will. Nothing's ever gonna change that, no matter what happens. We only got a last few days together, a matter of hours. That's gotta be enough for the both of us, Jackson, because there's nothing left beyond that. You know that in your own crazy way, just like I do in mine.

Lissa

There's one thing about Lem driving out to see Jackson that still affects me each time he goes, and that's how it's like I'm almost there with him for every passing mile.

I see him behind the wheel and I see Jackson waiting in his dilapidated house way out on that moonscape of a prairie, both of them with cigarettes in their fingertips and a far-off look in their eyes, both of them feeling like something is gaining on them and about to take over their lives. I don't think seeing your own brother should be such a charged event, but that's how it is for Lem — and now it is for me, too, through some kind of long-time osmosis. I don't worry about him getting in an accident or falling asleep at the wheel — I don't worry about any of the usual things people do when someone they care about takes off in the middle of the night for a family emergency, which is exactly what Jackson is and has been since they dragged him out of that cold icy water. I don't worry about these things.

What I worry about and what troubles me, so that I almost grieve over it, is that Lem somehow won't come back, not because he's driven away for good like his own father did but because Jackson has hurt or killed him. Lem doesn't want to believe that Jackson is capable of hurting him, but I know better — and not just because of what he did to those horses. I know it because I've seen it in his eyes. Jackson is a murderer. That's what Lem can't accept: that it doesn't matter what happened to Jackson to make him this way, all that matters is who and what he is now. He's a cold-blooded killer, even if he hasn't killed anyone yet. He certainly killed those poor horses. He admitted as much to me the night it was just the two of us. Maybe he wasn't born that way, and I didn't know him before he almost drowned, but he's a sociopath. And he's dangerous to everyone he comes across, whether there's a sad reason behind it or not.

I wish for everybody's sake, and maybe especially even for Jackson's, that he wasn't that way. But there's only one thing you can do with a killer, and that's to make sure he can't ever hurt anyone ever again by putting him behind bars for the rest of his life or putting him out of his own misery. I don't think there are any other alternatives. Nowadays they claim it's because of genes or DNA, but I'm not so sure: some human destinies can't be explained by science. Jackson is sitting in that clapboard house by himself, but it's like he's spiraling out to the darkest pits of space. He can't be saved — not by Lem, not by me, not by anybody. He thinks God is whispering in his ear and telling him what to do.

He killed those horses — and he hinted at things I can't forget, and I think that night he even considered doing something to me, going over it in his deranged mind. Lem gives him the power of clairvoyance, and I admit he sometimes says things that are eerily accurate and disturbing, even profound. But the devil himself is capable of that and a whole lot more. Jackson isn't even evil so much as lost in his own fantasy world of right and wrong, where he's the sole judge and arbiter, the only one who can decide. I don't care how much he wept about killing those horses, he still did it. He still had to think it

35

all out and execute them one by one, along with all the other grisly parts of it. I think he was testing himself. I think those horses were just the beginning of a bigger, more destructive plan.

Sometimes I don't think that Glendale is far enough away. There's nothing to keep him from driving out here to see us. I wish we were on the other side of the world. Scottie and Sam ask about him once in a while, but they know enough now not to pry. I look in Scottie's eyes sometimes, I try to see if I can see any trace of Jackson or his grandfather, if all the terrible things I've heard from Lem about growing up is somehow latent in Scottie. I feel shitty about that every time I look for it, like I don't trust my own son. I have to remind myself that for all of his faults, Lem's always been very gentle with me and the kids, to a fault, just mostly absent and ineffectual or quietly self-destructive. Even to this day he can hardly raise his voice to me, and God knows I've deserved it sometimes after what I've said to him, no matter how badly he's hurt me. Lem's completely whipped by the circumstances of his own life. Oddly enough, that makes him very docile and peaceful, almost meek. Once he couldn't keep playing baseball the way he used to he seemed to lose all confidence in other areas of his life. The only concrete and definitive decisions he ever makes involves his driving out to see Jackson when he gets in trouble. That's just about the only time he won't back down or compromise.

And so far Scottie's okay — I haven't seen any sign of Jackson in him so far. Or even much of Lem, for that matter.

Lem said he gave up drinking for me, but when I told him it can't work that way he looked like a whipped dog. I think he believed it would prove how serious he is about making this marriage work again. But it's not about that anymore. I can see a day when the kids will genuinely want to get to know him, when they'll gradually come to realize that whatever happened was a lot more complicated than they could ever imagine, but they're not there yet.

He needs to give them time, the same kind of time when he was away from them. You can't rush this kind of thing. So Lem goes from vice to vice, not out of malice or bitterness but because he doesn't know what else to do. He gave up drinking and tried to quit smoking, then he took up gambling. Finally he gave up gambling and started smoking again. Then when his knees and back got so bad, he got addicted to painkillers. I think at one time he was also addicted to one-night stands. If there's a little getaway in it, Lem Purchase will get hooked on it, as long as it give the promise of escape for a few hours. He goes from one to the other, never realizing they're all the same, just different in appearance.

Now I think he's addicted to an idea, the idea of getting back with me and seeing the kids more, though they live in their own places and I don't even see them every day. So what can you do with someone like that, someone you still care about but can't live with anymore, who suddenly sees all of us together like we're one big happy family? He likes to say I'm the best thing that ever happened to him, but I don't know if that's true: I could be one of the worst. I know I can be a royal bitch, and without much provocation either.

I've gotten so used to not having him around that even when we're together for two or three hours he about drives me up a wall. He's becoming a needy and fragile person — with a lot of legitimate aches and pains to go along with the undertow of his sorrow. Sometimes I just can't handle it. I don't want to handle it. I refuse to handle it. So I am a bitch. But I'm a bitch with wings, and I'm not about to give them up, not for Lem, not for Ray, not even for the kids. I'm growing stronger, and Lem is getting weaker. I don't want to waste this strength on someone who's only going to drag me down. I want to feel it for myself awhile, let it grow and expand inside of me. I don't care how selfish that sounds. I tried being the perfect wife and mother, and I'm through with all that. I'm just never going back there ever again.

37

The biggest thing now is Lem going out to see Jackson. I can't help worrying about it, and not because it brings back all the old fears and insecurities but because Jackson is getting worse with every passing month. He's off the charts with his apocalyptic visions, only a little of which Lem can bring himself to tell me about. But he doesn't have to say much because I can piece it together myself. Lem can overlook just about anything when it comes to Jackson, but I think even he is starting to get a little spooked. He even gave me a doctor's number nearby in Valentine, which he's never done before.

So this trip has a different feel to it all the way around. A lot is riding on it for everyone, both once he gets to Arrowhead and when he comes back. I wish I could spare him the grief of all this, the grief of seeing Jackson the way he is, and the grief I will have to give him when he comes home. But it can't be any other way now. Each one of us has passed the point of no return. So I guess we're all about to be tested, which I have to keep telling myself is an unavoidable part of moving forward, of being honest about how things really stand. The rest of it is just speculation.

I just want the phone to ring so he can tell me everything's okay. That's all I'm waiting for. Nothing has changed about that in twenty-five years. I keep telling myself that this is the last time, the very last, and then we can all move on. Otherwise it becomes just the old familiar routine, being held prisoner by what Jackson is going to do or has already done, or what he's talking about doing. Now it's finally time to make some plans of my own and actually follow through with them without apologizing to anyone, least of all to myself.

Jackson

Lissa knows. I almost didn't have to tell it to her, just breathe it out in code. She can decipher the dragons of my avowals as well as anyone. She's not a whore so much as she is a kind of chute through which different men pour their seeping grain. She's always known about me.

I was tempted to call her sister once before the word was snatched out of my mouth by a thunderclap. She didn't see Lem's horses as anything but victims. I tried to tell her about it, but then I stopped once I realized she couldn't hear me, when her eyes grew dark with frightened violets. But I told her anyway. She's sleeping with a man with a body like a train working up the side of a mountain, curving into the night. He laughs a lot, but there's no seeds in it. Lem is a cuckold. He walks around with the echoes of sweet cuts at B-P, the trajectory of hard line drives. He must be taught the truth and Lissa, too, but her time will have to wait.

When I blow things up the explosions speak beyond sound in the language of perilous flowers, in petals bright with the wings of angels. Then everything becomes a kind of glittering confetti drifting in the air. They call Nebraska the good life. But the good life has lost its meaning, its ability to stretch across the horizon like a woman lying breathless after lovemaking. I'm going to give it back to them in a way that will stun their hearts with fear, then cleanse them with solemn prayers. If there was another way I would surely do it.

When I shot the red horse it didn't go down so easily. It somehow moved the bullet around in its body, trying to find a place to spit it out. I laid my hand across the drum of its rib cage and it swelled and rumbled like a tremor deep inside the earth. I had to work fucking hard to make it dead. Shooting wasn't near enough. Its teeth were filled with malice and turned to me out of their thrashing caves in the walls of a collapsing kingdom. The ghost of a horse that's hard to kill is different than the others because part of its changing form has blowing dust in it that paints the air an ocher color with a little rust mixed in, a hue the air doesn't have by itself. You can taste the ghost of this horse on your tongue and it tastes like wind-driven sand, needle bright and gaining. It has never stopped knocking on the doors of my skin since I killed it. It wants to bury me alive. I can scatter it by waving my hands but I don't want resort to that. I just let it settle on my forehead and arms and later wash them off in swirling water going down the drain.

When I walked through the capitol building in Lincoln and gazed in wonder at all those earnest farmers and pioneers on the wall, when I saw the sprawling mural of how this land was settled along with the people this settling supplanted, I broke down in the middle of that sacred cathedral and they caught it all on camera. The security guard came up to me and asked me if something was wrong. I'm just saying good-bye, I told him, and he didn't know what I was talking about, like I knew he wouldn't. They had cameras that covered every sight line and angle and monitored the behavior of every visitor in high-definition, but those cameras can't see into your heart.

I wonder if you know what you're trying to secure,

I said to him, and then he got concerned. I talked to him in a calm, moderate voice bereft of malice, and asked him if he knew anything about combines or what fertilizer to use, and he stared at me dumbfounded.

What about Indians, do you know anything about them,

I asked, and stare-stare, his whole countenance dripped with it. I asked him who put the sky over all this land and what did it mean to him to walk around free under it, to be so free it's the gravest of all responsibilities, and a song in the soul you have to sing as praise or lament to God? And still, he gave me nothing but the hoops of his staring.

It's not that I was trying to teach him anything but that he had no interest in learning. *Sir, could you step outside with me,* and I said, Why, do my tears offend thee? — and *Sir, sir,* he kept saying sir, and I was quick to correct him. No, I said, it's not sir, it's the Lord, the Lord I'm talking about, and then another guard appeared behind the first and the security was all they knew along with the static of their one-ways. The security was everywhere, the security was all there was, even in the caverns of their mouths. But the Lord did not promise us such. *Do you know what you're protecting or why,* my voice getting louder so that other visitors started to look our way, a little gun-shy but curious all the same because I was starting to get under their skin in pinpricks of entertainment.

Listen, people of this dry goddamned place,

I shouted out and then they were on top of me. But my voice slipped between their arms like tumbling water. *See where our freedom came from,* I shouted, *what has happened to it now? Are these walls all that's left of it? Why did you come here today — to grieve like me?* And then they cuffed and muffled me.

If they only knew that the work I have been given to do is saying good-bye — if they only understood that love must be willing to go all the way into the mouth of the lion until it is the lion, then they would not have sought to silence me: they would have no need because we would be in kinship. But the security was all they wanted. And when the security is all people understand, then you must speak to them in the words they understand and that means fear and breach of that same security as a voice and an outcry, as only wreaking destruction can make sense to them now because they have already destroyed so much themselves through sloth, negligence, and catastrophic ignorance.

I was giving them one last chance to hear the truth and do something with it, but they would have none of it. That's why I was crying. They left only the deep sorrow of certainty in their shuddering eyes. I never wanted to be sure of anything — never wanted to be right.

Do you understand?

I always considered such desires the rickety dwelling places of cowards. But the security had turned them into ergonomic people who had orgasms according to a daily planner, who went into the sarcophagi of tanning beds and sat for days on end in front of screens, waiting to be told about what to want and what to be and how fucking happy they were going to be someday, what they should dream about when they fell asleep and what they should think about when they were awake. I cried and reached out to them one last time as lost brothers and sisters but their ciphershood could not be filled with understanding. They didn't want real freedom. They wanted it in a brochure or under glass, where they could not touch it for fear of germs and bird flu.

I waited for my fellow citizens to come to my rescue, to give the slightest drizzling shit, but they just stood there with crumbs of birthday cake stuck between their teeth. So that's how it was and how it had to be. Even the old people looked like teenagers in their blinding white tennis shoes. But once they see the Sower falling out of the sky they'll begin to understand. They'll see his lightning-dented copper eyes and learn how to weep some honest goddamned tears. This is the best hope they have. It's all I have to give them.

Long ago the Sioux used to put their dead in trees, and some nights you can still hear them moaning if you learn how to be like grass. To put the body of someone you love wrapped up in animal hides in the limbs of a tree is an offering that celebrates the whole earth. Then even decay is lifted off the ground and the air knows what to do with it. If there are scavengers they must look up at what they intend to scavenge, and looking up is prayer. Can't be otherwise. All I want them to do is look up. Look up into the sky. You can bow your heads later on. But now it's time to look up. Because you can almost see it or imagine that it's there. The people we love slowly turning into light, nursing the grief and sorrow in order for the light to liberate them. We're made of wind just like they are. The feathers that decorate our bones are beautiful, made for flying and holding the light in a radiant way. What other song is there? But first you need the dead to put in trees. Then the rest will follow, and we can do the work of redemption. That's all that God asks of us, all that He requires.

Lem

I don't mind failing. I was a career .280 hitter, if that's any indication. One year I hit .320 halfway through the season before I blew out my knee in three different places. I wasn't what you'd call a power hitter, but I could turn doubles into triples and steal bases at will. If I got on, you could pretty much mark it down in the run column almost every time. Once in a while I'd hit one out, but that was fairly rare. No one tried to run on me because I had the best arm in AAA from center field, probably as good as anyone in the bigs at the time. So as a prospect coming up I had a few things going for me — speed, a Clemente-like arm, solid hitter, and potential in the power department with my frame and size, kind of like Andy Van Slyke, who played for the Pirates with Barry Bonds before Bonds became a freakish lab experiment. I think I could have grown into power the way a lot of players beef up today, even without the temptation of steroids.

But I never had the chance to find out.

It doesn't make me bitter so much as wonder what might have been, which I know doesn't do a damn bit of good. But still I wonder about it sometimes, especially when I'm out on the road driving like this, trying to keep my mind off Jackson or my own personal family and financial woes. I just naturally drift back to the possibilities of those days and the occasional flashes of fulfillment. If my spikes hadn't caught the way they did it might have been a whole different story because I was on my way toward being called up in August: Harum even told me so a week before the injury. The double irony of the whole damn thing is I had the base stolen easily, I could have gone in standing up. But some things are so ingrained you can't do it any other way.

You see these old ballplayers hanging around the ballpark sometimes, at least I do, and they have this kind of slouch about them, I don't know how else to describe it: something about the way their shoulders pinch inward, leaning over a fence down the third base line or over a beer at the bar with their thin hairy arms. It's more than getting old, it's like they've been cheated or someone took something from them and they've just started to realize it. I've always wondered about that slouch, if it's not somehow a sign of those who played the game and were any good at it, especially as I'm becoming one of those old-timers myself.

I remember watching Ted Williams throw out his last pitch at Fenway, and to this day I wish I'd never seen it: there he was, the old Splendid Splinter himself, a genuine American hero in every sense of the word, all jowly and trembling, throwing to the plate like a grandmother and trying not to embarrass himself with big sloppy tears in his eyes. Geriatric, that's how he looked, which is putting it mildly. I think it was unnecessary, but you know how it is: people love a spectacle. It probably even made some people feel good to see a great athlete like Ted Williams reduced to age spots and facial tics he couldn't control. But these old guys I'm starting to notice, they hardly miss a thing peering out from under their caps and visors. They must have shown up on my radar screen at some point, because suddenly they've been popping up everywhere I go.

It's not that I never thought I'd become one of them, I just didn't give them much thought either way. But now I see them all over, hanging around the games I scout with this detached kind of interest that's almost like sadness only minus the hysterics, like winning or losing isn't even the issue anymore, if it ever truly was.

Lately I've been wondering about success stories in America, whether it's in sports, business, or the movies. Like everyone else I want to ask, How'd they do it? What's the secret? But it's more than that: I want to know how has-beens like me could get to the threshold and be right there knocking on the door, with about as much talent as anyone, only for whatever reason something happened and we didn't get our shot, or we blew the shot we did get, which is probably more than most people can say. I don't know. That's why it keeps coming back to me.

I think about Jackson and how we grew up, how he wasn't always the way he is now, what a bitch that is all the way around, and how nobody can do a damned thing about it, including me. Things used to be so easy, they just came right up with open arms inviting me in, saying, *Come on, you're one of us,* whether it was sports, women, or the admiration of others. It doesn't mean I didn't work my tail off or didn't appreciate them, but I have to admit, they came pretty easily there for awhile, especially at first, like apples falling from a tree.

Why me?

I'd sometimes ask in surprise,

Why have I been given so much and someone like Jackson has these mental challenges and all the rest of it?

Somewhere along the way that question slowly changed, I'm not even sure when it happened, and the questions became Why *not* me? Why didn't I make it? Where did it all go wrong? Was I fooling myself or just hearing what I wanted to hear?

It's not just blowing out my knee that night in Oklahoma City, not the drinking or problems with Lissa — not the hundred and one things that everyone has to face eventually. It doesn't matter who you are, it's just that odd, persistent question that sounds almost like a voice crying in the dark, Why didn't I make it? Where did things go wrong? I'm not even that upset about it anymore, but I keep asking out of curiosity and even wonder. I mean, where in the hell did it all go so fast — the promise and the potential and the ability to bounce back from injury and adversity and everything else? Sooner or later questions like those are gonna find you no matter where you are, they're gonna get you in a corner and they're not gonna let up their interrogation at all, rising up off the road you're driving on, like a thunderhead towering in the distance that you're heading straight into.

I remember one night in the early days, this woman came up to me in a bar after a game, just like Lissa did at that party in Pasadena when we first met. I'd gone two for four, stolen a couple of bases, it was a good outing. I was whipped and didn't even want to go out that night, but Lucious Grimes kept ragging on me and finally I just gave in. We weren't there more than twenty minutes when this beautiful, knock-out of a woman — I mean she was a real stunner by anyone's standards, dark hair all the way down her back, a body with impossible curves about to bust out all over — comes up to me and starts pouring it on. I in no way encouraged the situation or was even looking for it.

Her name was Jan or Jane, I forget which, and she was a stewardess from Sante Fe there for one more night, and I don't know why she chose me, but she did. The Eagles were playing in the background and I was looking into her Elizabeth Taylor eyes thinking, Well, I better make a choice here, and I know what the right choice is, but Lissa was a thousand miles away in California nursing Scottie and it had been a brutal road trip, the kind where you're sore all over, everything smells like a jockstrap, and this meter in my head I didn't even realize was there had been ticking right along, counting up a hundred thousand things all that time. Suddenly it just clicked into place: this was a bonus out of the blue being offered to me, a beautiful, brief, one-night bonus. It was like someone had tapped me on the shoulder and said, Lem, this is part of it, the life you've chosen or that's chosen you. Enjoy it while you can.

So I did.

I started to enjoy it. I didn't go out of my way looking for it, but I didn't exactly avoid it either. I put myself where things were happening, and they did. Slowly at first, but once I got rolling there was no stopping me. I was the last one out of the bar and the first one at the batting cage, and that's how I justified it. Didn't seem to have any effect on the field, as far as I could tell. I knew I loved Lissa and that my life was with her, and I'm not just saying that now to cover my ass, but it was true and it's still true today: she wasn't like any of the women I slept with on the road, who all kind of merged into one laughing woman with a sandal dangling from the end of her painted toenails and a drink in her hand.

What the hell do you expect when you're away from home for six or seven months out of the year, living out of planes and buses and motel rooms in twenty different states? What did anyone expect? There was just one guy on our team, a second baseman from Indiana by the name of Herm Calvert, who was married and never went astray as far as I could tell. He couldn't hit a lick and was balding even then, but he had a pretty good glove and was just eking out the last of his playing days between AA and AAA, sometimes filling in at other positions as a utility player: he knew his days were numbered while the rest of us didn't. Or maybe we just couldn't admit it to ourselves. The rest of us were too young and wild to have the foggiest idea of what was in store for us. But somehow ol' Herm had made peace with the crucial and important fact that he wasn't going to make it and hadn't even come close, that he'd end his playing days somewhere in Iowa in front of a crowd of fifty people after a twelve-hour bus ride, just like where he'd started ten years before. Somehow he was okay with that.

I started to call him Preacher, only I have no idea whether he was religious or not as he hardly said a word. But Herm read all the time, which was a pretty rare thing in that environment, unless it was *Playboy* or *Sports Illustrated* — and one day when I looked over his shoulder to see what he was reading I saw that it was basic accounting, of all things. He was preparing for life after baseball — I guess he'd been preparing all along. Once I started calling him Preacher the name just stuck and that's what everyone called him — and he became like this kind of beloved mascot, I don't know how else to describe it. The name Preacher just fit him for some reason. I only had one serious conversation with Preacher that I remember, during a rain delay in Toledo. He was picking mud out of his spikes with a screwdriver at the end of the bench and I went up to him and started asking him a few things.

Preacher,

I said, What do you get out of playing anyway? I mean, what the hell are you doing still hanging on the way you do?

To this day I have no idea why I had the balls to talk to him that way. But Preacher looked up at me calmly, not really surprised or put out or even annoyed, and he said something I'll never forget, he said

Because it's the purest thing I know. And I won't be able to do it forever.

Then he went back to picking mud out of his spikes. And Preacher, Herm Calvert from French Lick, Indiana, was right, he was dead-on — baseball is a pure game if you play it right, and you can become pure, too, at least when you're between the lines. I came to need those lines badly, because things only made sense between them, even when I wasn't hitting: it was outside of them that everything started to unravel. Things come back to you, they really do. No matter how clichéd that sounds, they eventually find their way back and there's nothing you can do about it but recognize it when they come and take what's been waiting for you all along. That's what happened to Mickey Mantle and a hundred others I could name, including myself. No matter how good or promising we were, we somehow always ended up in some sorry, pathetic state, the same exact one I was in until just about a year ago. And I'm not out of the woods yet.

I think there's a myth that surrounds a certain type of ballplayer, the ones with the most ability and the biggest appetites — the ones who lived extra-colorful lives to match their abilities, like the Babe or any number of them. I'm not comparing myself to them, you understand, but I know the territory all right. This is how you do it, they seemed to say, only they never had to say a word because it's who and what they were that did all the talking. If they did talk they backed it up, which just added to their legend. Then there are the others, like me, the ones who got a little taste of glory, who were there for a second or two before it was taken away from us. We have a story, too, but it's not the one you hear about every day, maybe because people don't especially want to hear it. I know I didn't until it happened to me.

We are the has-beens and the washouts and ne'er-do-wells, the ones who almost made it and didn't for a thousand different reasons under the sun, both bogus and legit. Some of us are bitter and some of us are lost, but all of us are bewildered at what our lives have become, trying to find a little place in the big bad sea that finally swallowed us up. I'm starting to see these kinds of guys everywhere I go and it scares the shit out of me, because I know they spend most of their lives in gloomy sports bars, talking with their cronies who give them a sense of who they used to be. We're almost like the backbone of this country, the ones who watch the others do what we never could quite pull off or sustain.

Jackson, who a lot of people consider the royal fuck-up to end all fuck-ups, seems to understand this better than anyone, even better than me: he understands it so well, he's the only person I know who can give a voice to it, who can somehow put it in a way that makes so much searing sense it's almost unbearable. Jackson *knows* things and I have no clue why: it's just this odd, burning gift he has, this strange ability to cut through all the bullshit and get right to the heart of the disease. Maybe that's why I drive out to him like I do, for some kind of goddamned, shrieking clarity I can't get otherwise, even if what I end up seeing and hearing isn't exactly pretty. I say I'm trying to save him, but maybe it's me I'm trying to save. I never realized this about myself before coming out this one last time.

He talks about the heartland of America like he's inside its soul somehow, like he's been there all along and absorbed all the important lessons most everyone else has forgotten or don't even know about. He understands what I tried to do and failed in doing, and how it has cost me dearly in the things that matter most, the people I neglected but never stopped loving, even for a second while I was away. I wish people could know this about him, could catch a glimpse of what he says that isn't all just out-and-out insanity, though I can't follow him half the time. He's the only family I got left apart from Lissa and the kids, who don't hardly even know me.

It's like this ongoing argument I keep having with myself, like I'm pulled in opposite directions — not because I want to cut Jackson any slack (there's just no wiggle room anymore after what he said in that last call) but just to recognize with some kind of honesty what's really going on here. How it's not an open-and-shut case when you're coming out to say good-bye to your brother who's gone off the deep end. Maybe not all of Jackson is lost and crazy but something else is, something tiny and precious and good, maybe something even necessary.

I'm probably the last person in the world who understands this, Jackson's last thread of connection to human contact or sense of reality. And I'm gonna do the only thing I can do now, but first I gotta see him one last time. He said he loved the horses he killed but that he had to kill them for me because he loved me even more. As fucked-up as this sounds, I believe him somehow: I believe he thought he had to do those awful things because it was a test he had to pass. That's what Jackson thinks, that's why he could follow through with what he did. I'm not saying it was right, that those horses deserved it — all I'm saying is that's where he was coming from. Nothing's ever just one way, never what it seems. There's always an angle to it that no one else can see. Jackson's crazy, but he's my brother. I can't help it if nobody understands that. I don't even understand it myself.

He talks about the kingdom sometimes, he talks about an aura and an after-glow, like a far-off ball of trembling light getting closer all the time. I used to think it was because of what he saw when his heart quit beating that cold winter day when they dragged him out of the tank. But now I'm not so sure. He's got the fervor of religion flowing in his veins now, convictions that nobody can put a dent in, let alone explain. He thinks America has to be destroyed in order to come back again. He thinks it's Armageddon time, that he's some messenger of God. Sometimes when I look into his sky blue eyes and hear him go off the way he does, I almost want to believe him — I almost think he's not delusional or as sick as he is, that maybe he's onto something.

He knows what's killing me. He knows I'm trying to get well. He knows how I ended up the way I did, estranged from my wife and kids and a recovering alcoholic and addict galore of painkillers, still in love with the same dream that won't ever come true, my own ball of trembling blue fire that has burned up most of my life. I don't know how he knows it, living out in that tiny crumbling house all by himself, fifteen minutes from where we grew up. But he does, and he tells me about it in his quiet, high-up voice, like grass getting brushed out by the wind sweeping across the plains all the way from Canada, like he can read people's hearts and minds — mine, Lissa's, the kids', the woman at the supermarket check-out line's, the president, anyone he cares to focus on. It's not even about baseball anymore. Maybe it never was. It was about becoming somebody, becoming someone who the ones you love could look up to and admire, that you yourself could look up to — and coming up so high and dry and empty, it's like you lost your soul in the process.

Then I remember those mutilated horses and I think there's just no way, I can't let myself go down that road. I know what I should have done a long time ago and didn't because I was holding out the wildest kind of chance that he'd somehow turn it around, but it never happened. So now I have to. He's my brother, but I have to. There's no turning back now. It's one way for Jackson and me, for all of us. What happens after I betray and turn my brother in, I don't know. I don't want to know. I don't even want to think about it.

Lissa

So how did Jackson do it, how did he keep me in that room all night with thunder in the distance and Lem not knowing I was there, while he told me what he did to those horses, how he got them to come in closer and closer until he captured them and slaughtered them one by one? And why did he want to tell it to me as if I alone could understand what it meant and why he thought he had to do it?

Why?

Because what Jackson said that night follows me everywhere I go, into buildings and crowded shops and the back rooms of restaurants where people are laughing at the next table, and even when I'm on top of Ray loving him for all he's worth. Jackson is leaning down into my face with his hands on the arms of the chair like he was about to kiss me, telling me about the horses going down into the smoldering ground so that something bright and shining could rise up out of their smoking ashes where he had slaughtered them.

I sat there, I listened to him, my hands folded in my lap like a little girl. I barely allowed myself to breathe. How he went about describing it with such calm deliberation and even pride is the reason I couldn't break away or interrupt him, I couldn't bring myself to tell him to stop it, Please just stop it — because I wanted to see and hear for myself how he would finish the telling of it, if he got upset or showed any remorse or doubt or even sadness. But I didn't hear or see even a hint of these in his voice or his face, they just didn't factor in to what he felt he'd been commanded to do and how he went about telling it to me. Then I knew I'd been right about Jackson all along, that he really did believe he was the messenger of God or his instrument or some other far-fetched harrowing thing. But I needed to hear all of it in order to confirm what I already knew about him that Lem couldn't bring himself to believe. I didn't tell Lem about it because I couldn't. I didn't tell anyone. All I wanted was to never see Jackson again after that night and I haven't, and neither have the kids.

Secrets can grow in people's hearts like dark blooming flowers, because that's part of their power. They can take on draperies of shadows that lilt and fill up with wind to droop back down though they're always there, waiting to fill up again and assume their proper size. At first I wanted to tell someone, anyone, about what Jackson had told me: I wanted to shout it out and cry and sob, but I couldn't bring myself to do it. I started to call 911 before I hung up because it went so far down into me that words couldn't touch it, like Jackson had put his shaking, oily finger on a part of my soul. And I had to let him do it, I had to sit there and let him tell it to the end. There was just no other way.

So does that make me an accomplice to Jackson's crime, even though those horses were already dead when he told me about them? Did my listening signal my acceptance and even approval? Can you hear something like that and in the act of hearing it somehow condone and be a part of it?

I thought if I was quiet and still enough then what he was saying couldn't touch me or anyone else I cared about, couldn't travel like wind-blown dust all the way to California to be breathed in by Scottie and Sam while they slept, like so many millions of others who didn't know about the reality of people like Jackson Purchase. These are people so lost and abandoned and sick that they set up kingdoms in their heads that always turn to violence and destruction sooner or later because that's where their dream worlds take them. They don't or can't acknowledge that there are hurt and raging people sprinkled all across America, some of them so bitter and lost they want to lash out and hurt someone, anyone, even some wild horses that wandered in from eastern Colorado one day like clouds drifting across the horizon.

Jackson turned those horses into a sign and that's why he killed them, because he thought they were meant just for him: he took possession of them in his mind and turned them into pawns in his own sick cosmic game. That's one of the reasons why all I want anymore is to see things as they really are — people picking out apples at the supermarket, a teenage girl combing her hair in front of a rear view mirror, an old man walking his Pekinese dog — precious, ordinary, humming things like that.

I don't want imagination anymore, I don't need it. I lived through it with Lem all those years with what could or should have been. That was enough for me. I have this thing with Ray now, and I didn't have to dream about it because suddenly it was just there. I'm starting to love my life in a way I couldn't before and none of these, not even the first cup of coffee in the morning in the kitchen by myself, has anything to do with imagination.

That's what I realized about Jackson, listening to him that night the way I did: imagination is all he has left, the last and only thing. Everything else real about him has been swept away by madness. That's why he's so dangerous. Lem is a dream addict, which is probably where all his other addictions come from. But only he can wake himself up. The kids are grown now. They're young adults. Sam is a beautiful young woman with a mind of her own, Scottie is tall and straight, quiet like Lem but with clear green eyes. He doesn't drink at all. He's working on a business degree at UC Irvine, he'll graduate in three and a half years. They're not dreamers, and every day I'm very thankful for that. God save us from the dreamers. I want to see where their lives take them, which is nothing anyone can imagine. I gave up on speculation a long time ago. There's nothing to justify or explain. I love them but I've let them go. Lem loves them too, but he can't let them go, though he never really had them to begin with.

Jackson said there's a brightness that's calling him. His eyes grew narrow, like sparkling pins, when he said it. I always believed brightness was a good thing, the way it can fill up a window or break out from under a door, a thousand small and heartbreaking things, the greatest hope there is or can be, a baby being born. But for Jackson brightness is different — for him it's the brightness of catastrophe, like the end of the world in a far-off explosion. He believes in a brightness that can blind you, that can sweep you out of this world in a whirlwind.

I let him tell me about it, tell me all the ways brightness has been calling him since the day he almost drowned, the melting and wavering light high above the water. God, death, and brightness became mixed up in his head. I want to say I pity him, but I'd be lying: I didn't know him the way he was before. I only know him the way he is now. He thinks they were Lem's horses and that he was destined to kill them. He thinks their ghosts are still around, haunting his house, circling for him at night. All I could do was listen in spite of myself. It was like hearing the initiation ritual of a killer who hadn't yet killed, who practiced first on wild horses.

You want to do something when you hear it, hold up your hand, say, *No, I refuse to hear this, I refuse to let you go on this way,* but I didn't. I never did. But there's another kind of brightness not even Jackson knows, the glowing and broken truth that's waiting for each one of us. I'm going to share the knowledge of this with Lem when he gets back. I have to. Then maybe something good can come out of all of this. I have to believe it; I have no choice. Otherwise this will just keep going on and on and on until Jackson does something that nobody, not even Lem, can excuse him for.

Jackson

It's a breathable countdown we're talking about now as I'm stationed here at the window with my palm on the stock of the M24 that will buck, sleek and bone-jarring, in the cradle of my shoulder when it comes time to cut loose. The others are lined up within easy reach, like the ribs of a prehistoric carnivore skinned for thread-bare display: eleven in all, different calibers and muzzle velocities. Some are so well made they look like the bare outlines of a new world order, ready to shoot tracers deep into the night. I came in my own hand the last time four weeks ago and wrote it down on an old index card. Then I drank my final beer and crushed the can underfoot to seal the deal. Since then I've forsaken myself in order to be pure, though only a teenage Christ with peach fuzz on his cheeks can truly pull that off.

These are the days of teeming last things, every one of them shining rapt and unbearable, just like I knew they would be.

I saw it all happening in my dreams a thousand times before as I sat here, dizzy with vindication. At the end of every dream it's time to wake up, and that's where we as a nation are headed now. The rest of them will have to join me in this stark and radiant knowledge. I haven't moved from the window except to take care of the urgencies of my body, and then I take care of business as quickly as I can. I don't linger over my own waste. I still have a few Pall Malls, but at this rate they won't even last up to the moment of my death two or three nights hence when I drive into Lincoln with my load. Smoke is the only thing I sup on now. Only the cricket under the porch will survive the conflagration to come, the holocaust of the heartland. This is why I love it beyond all measure, just like God does.

Even Lem's horses are powerless to stop what's coming, though they give it a numinous weight and form in the hue of a drifting miasma that smells here and there like gunpowder and a few cast-off fuel injectors. I need their outraged spirits as a way of keeping awake, more than any flavor crystals. Lem is a pair of headlights blooming in the night, their halogen death rays a stare and a baptism, so help me, the one true brimming Lord. I can see him fiddling with the dial to catch up on the latest scores or whitewash bullshit in Washington, but what he mostly hears is the static between stations and voices crying out from an FM wilderness, so hollow and abject they outline the void itself with a veneer of comic rejoinders.

I figure he's a few hundred miles out and closing fast, his steel-belted Goodyears worn down to a threadbare Aztec design. He's coming with a Judas kiss, but I'm the one who will purse my lips and cry, rocking him in my arms for the final time. I don't have to bless what I see anymore and the visions I have because they're stamped in my blood like a burning book. I've been living on peanut butter and corn chips lately, until they gave out five days ago; since then it's been the fumes of Lem's horses and the rest of my Pall Malls. I've dwindled down to the size of a penlight searching the night for anything it can find. Lem will feel the magnetic field of my hunger when he arrives. It will hum around him like a downed power line, its needle pointing north, and then we can face the truth that's been waiting for us all along.

They won't call it love in the history books but that's exactly
what it is. Only love understands the need for sacrifice and for
fire. I never wanted to hurt anyone, but it's rising up inside of
me, the unspeakable task I've been given to carry out with a son's
steadfast loyalty. Part of it will involve my own smoking corpse.
One of the horses tried to drift through the keyhole, wraith-like,
an hour ago, but I banished it with an improvised flamethrower
comprised of Lysol and a strike from my well-used Zippo and the
heel of my hand. The horse curled up properly and turned back
on its rearing haunches made of outraged vapor. They're always
trying to get in here to stomp the life out of me, but I smell them
coming in — then I torch them in the livid air.

You were young and promising once, Lem, and so was I. The
future was laid out before us in rippling purple grains of majesty.
Remember how Mama used to bake on Sunday afternoons while
we sat around the house, indolent as butterflies? All she wanted
was to love and take care of us, and we fit that bill all right. Then
playing long toss and shagging fly balls down at Groves Field. I tell
you, brother, those days come back to me as the best times I ever
had. Oh, Lem, I don't want to kill you but neither did Abraham
with Isaac. I love you, brother, but it's time to say good-bye. You
think you have to betray me for my own good, but it doesn't work
that way and never could. I'll make sure it's clean and fast, you
won't hardly feel a thing for the shock of it. I'll hold your hand
till the end.

You're my brother, brother, and that means I have to be the
steward of your death. Only Lissa knows how sick you are, but she
can't bring herself to admit it. It would mean a complete upheaval
of all she knows and believes in. She doesn't see that most everyone
is sick in America today, but I see it in their eyes at Wal*Mart and
Auto Zone and all the places where people think they're safe or
saved or get some kind of goddamned guarantee.

Did this nation really think its whorish excesses could be sustained?

But you and I know better, don't we, Lem: we paid our big-time dues in the betrayal of our ideals that were stripped away from us one by one, the shards of broken promises and dreams, you as a ballplayer and me as an ex-soldier among a thousand other smoking pieces still smoldering on the ground. America turned its back on us and millions of others just like us and moved on to the next wide-eyed sucker. But you were beloved, Lem, you had it all once, what people looked up to and wanted to be, I more than any other as your little brother, the one that liked to tag along. I watched it from close up and from afar. You couldn't know what that was like because you were too busy being adored.

Now that adoration's got to be paid for.

You've reached the limit of your luck and magic is all. It's not your fault, Lem. It was bound to happen sooner or later. Couldn't be any other way. We'll go out together in a blaze of infamous glory, only the order will be reversed, which won't mean a thing next to the forever that's waiting for us. I'll kill you out of mercy, Lem, I'll kill you because that's the last and greatest gift I could ever give to you, to make sure they always remember you as a hero and a martyr, a fireman running into a burning building never to come out again.

Never mind when I drowned for you, it's time to forego water now for fire. But I'll be able to touch you and close your eyelids and kiss the crags of your forehead. Maybe we'll even smoke a last cigarette together, from your lips to mine then back again, before your eyes circle the drain and the light goes out of them for good. I wonder if you have any idea how much you mean to me, how precious the least thing is about you. I see you as God must see you, a troubled miracle with iridescent eyes that used to be able to read the spinning seams of a slider at eighty-five miles an hour. That last bullet will be my parting hymn to you; I'll be following close behind. The rest of it's already paid for in Christ's blood.

The infrared night goggles are good to go, clear as diving into the waters off Corpus Christi. They must be my eyes and ears now, the ones that will pick you up first, that will register the least particle of your body heat. Not a single breath of yours shall go unrecorded, I promise you. You're a bundle of data now bereft of memory and longing, but I'll supply the nostalgia and the heart-break. Don't you worry about that. You'll never be just a node of information to me, brother, a heat sensor moving across a screen. I would never do you like that.

If we had time, brother, if we had just one more day or week beyond our appointed hour, I'd lay it all out before you and try to explain it down to the last aching detail, after all this agony and ecstasy, which aren't worth a shit unless they lead to a national rebirth and transcendence. You'll be a martyr and I'll be the villain and the scapegoat, the one they'll say went off the deep end like Koresh down in Waco. I can already hear them lining up to pass judgment on me: if he could kill his own brother, if he could resort to such a thing, if he could plan it all out to the last craven detail, if he could even conceive of it with innocent women and children caught in the crossfire.

But you'll be a hero, Lem, just like you always were to me, only the seismic effect will ripple across the entire country now, with millions and millions of people whispering your name. We'll be the stark everlasting power struggle every American will be able to understand, and I want you to be the good one, I want you to be the hero. I'm gonna make you immortal, Lem, I'm gonna make sure they remember and think of you forever. All your other faults and failures will be forgiven but not forgotten, to magnify your selflessness, just like Lincoln's. I've dreamed and planned for this day for years, I've it orchestrated down to your last dying speech, which I already know word for word.

Why, Jackson? Why are you doing this?

Because I love you, brother, I love you more than you love yourself. It was always this way. You never did manage to get your name up in lights, so here's your opportunity to be in every history book in America from now on, Lemmuel Purchase, the ex-ballplayer who died at the hands of his own brother trying to save innocent lives. Then you'll be redeemed, and no one, not even Lissa, will be able to take that away from you. I died in that icy pond so that you could live, but you went and blew it all to hell. I knew I'd have to kill you so that you could be immortal.

They'll do everything to justify their sloth and ignorance, the selfishness that led to this crucial moment in history. Because history is rationalization on a colossal scale, American history no different than any other. I wanted so badly to think it was, I held out longer than anyone else with what I knew, but I came round eventually to that hard and brutal fact. I had to. It's the same old bullshit wrapped up in the stars and stripes, attracting its own panoply of snarling flies. So that's where we are, brother, the needle point about to Geiger over into another 9-11, only homegrown this time.

I'm banking on the headlong nature of your restlessness, the one that's made you know the highways of America as well as any trucker strung out on No-Doz. You've never been behind the wheel so much as you have always been a part of it. If Lissa only knew it wasn't women or booze she had to worry about but long distance, then maybe you two would have had a chance. I was pulling for you to make it, though Lissa was always afraid of me. I wasn't much of an uncle to your kids, but most families aren't much interested in the truth, just making sure they get their own and maintaining it. Fuck everybody else. That's why they got to suffer sometimes. I don't know if I could have taught them anything, but I would have opened my arms to them and loved them like my own. I hope you know that, brother — and even if you don't, I'm saying it here and now at the glowing end of my cigarette, once and for all.

It's quiet here, Lem, so quiet I can hardly believe what's about to
go down that I'm the primary author of, under God's own shining
decree. I love this fucking country and that's why I gotta do this.
You know that better than anyone, even if you can't hang it up in
words. We both do. I loved America so much I couldn't pretend
I didn't see what was happening. I would have died for it a dozen
times over, but I guess only once will have to do. Better men than
I have tried.

You'll know soon enough why I studied all those cloud for-
mations when we were kids and why they were so dear to me. I
was seeking to read the will of God in the language He chose to
speak to me, even if I didn't know it for thirty years and it took
me all that time to decipher what He was telling me to do. When
the truck goes off we'll both already be dead, which has got to be
some kind of consolation. The Sower will fall out of the sky, his
giant copper head like a meteorite with its own crown of thorns.
Then the ensuing bewilderment and mayhem will pave the way for
change, the last chance this country has to get back to what made
it great. Otherwise it has no future — not because of people like
me or Arabs flying into skyscrapers or blowing themselves up on
buses, but because it's getting eaten away from the inside by its own
self-made cancer and talk shows, the trivia that's turned it into one
vast amusement park of the motherfucking living dead.

Believe me, brother, and mark my words: more than a few will
understand; more than a few will see the necessity for it, trailing
years, decades, and wars behind, why it had to be this way, dear
brother, with your clueless innocence leading the way so that I can
be the guilty one they will eventually come to recognize as their
reluctant savior, the one who took them into the valley of death
so they could raise each other up above it where they were always
meant to be.

Lem

I've got all these things I want to say to you, Jackson. I've rehearsed them over and over a hundred times in a hundred different ways, but I know when I actually get there and see you face to face they'll evaporate into the air above us and I'll have to start over from square one, just like I always do.

It's the damndest thing to me, you seem to hijack my tongue every time I lay eyes on you. I guess that's just the way it's gotta be for now. As long as I don't start drinking again and you don't hurt anyone, everything will turn out all right. I have to believe that, and you should, too. I don't want what I have to say to sound like an ultimatum, but I can't control how it sounds anymore. I'll be speaking for other people now when I say the things I gotta say and follow through with, even little kids and babies that haven't yet been born.

So that's a whole new level right there.

I feel it pressing down on me with every passing mile, past the neon lights of Carson City and all the staring cactus, the gravity of what has to be done and all that it involves. God help me and guide me by His polished stars. I couldn't go back on it now, even if

I wanted to. You've got to realize that somewhere in your unsettled mind. And if I can't make you see it, then no one can. It's the purity of my motive that concerns me now. That's all I've got to go on. But Jesus, Jackson, there's so much to be thankful for and happy about, so much to celebrate in this wide open and free country of ours, in our very own lives.

I saw the sunrise sober for the first time in over thirty years just a couple of months ago: up till then the only time I saw one was when I was drunk or just coming out of one. I even talked to Scottie almost a whole hour on the phone the other day. Can you believe that? That's a record for us: we never talked that much before, let alone on the phone. And it wasn't even what we said so much as the tone of our conversation and how we listened to each other. It's the *pauses* that rocked me, that almost brought me to my knees. I can't hardly believe I'm their father and they still love me after all I did and didn't do, the zero presence I used to be in their lives. I can't afford to take them for granted ever again.

I've come to realize after all these years that what I love the most was always right there in front of me, waiting for me to come home, but I was too busy chasing after a dream that would never come true and just about did me in, which is exactly what I deserved. At least I know the truth now, and being sober gives me focus and clarity so I'm not about to forget it. I'm not going back to the way I was, waking up in strange motel rooms with someone I picked up at a bar, or dead drunk alone with cotton mouth and a sour stomach, staring up at the ceiling and feeling like the lowest kind of shit. Or driving drunk with a case of beer in the backseat and a can open and cradled between my legs, spilling all over my crotch, not giving a damn. It's a flat-out miracle I didn't kill anyone or myself. I've woken up staring at so many ceilings in so many different rooms with the highway traffic flying by outside I can hardly bear to think of it.

But that's over now, I've put it all behind me. Doesn't mean I don't want a drink something fierce sometimes, doesn't mean I'm not tempted to break my resolve nearly every damn day: that sudden overwhelming urge can crop up anywhere, anytime, like some demonic jack-in-the-box. I can hardly believe how strong it is when it does. But I have something to live for now, Jackson, something I care about more than baseball or my own selfish dreams. So it's one day at a time, one day at a time, and sometimes not even that: one minute, one hour, the very next second, half a second. I'm an aging father and I have responsibilities that I've let slide for too long now. You can only rely on benign neglect for so long. My kids need me even if they don't know it right now, even if I've been dead to them for decades. I refuse to believe it's too late. Talking with Scottie the other night gave me hope to think everything's gonna somehow be okay.

Sam, you'd hardly believe how beautiful and independent she's become. She looks just like Lissa who, I swear to God, has never looked better. That's a cruel form of payback if there ever was one, but I deserve every last bit of it. I thought women were supposed to lose their looks faster than men, but it's like she's coming into a second bloom. And I'd like to be there with her all the way. I just think it takes men a helluva lot longer to learn the most basic things, but this time I can honestly say I've learned what I need to know to go forward and be a good husband for her.

I think if you got out of Arrowhead the world might open up for you a little bit, give you a little crease of daylight to glimpse the possibilities of what your life can be. You're not that old. Even if you had to go somewhere for awhile where you'd be taken care of and monitored, you'd have a good shot at recovery. Anything's possible if there's love and a helping hand involved. I wouldn't be driving out here clean and sober if that wasn't the case. That's all I want for you, Jackson. And it's not just because you're my brother. I think you're a unique human being with some special gifts who just got sidetracked and fucked-up something fierce along the way. No one knows about that damage better than I do because I was there for a good part of it. I've tried to tell that to Lissa but she doesn't have ears to hear me right now. It's not her fault, and I don't blame her. The whole horse incident would spook anyone. It spooked me pretty good myself.

She's afraid of you, but she doesn't know the whole story because the whole story can't be put into words. It can never be put into words. It's more than getting you the help you need. I think you also need to talk with someone who might even share some of your radical views, so you can let loose of some of the pressure you've built up inside. Someone who'd be willing to listen to all that you have to say no matter how disturbing it is. It just can't be me anymore. So there's no need to rule out anything at this point.

My biggest hope and wish for you is that you'll come to see and accept what I'm saying — not because I'm the one who's saying it but because you'll see and understand for yourself that's it got to be this way if you're ever gonna have a chance. Then things can happen the way they're supposed to. We've spent so much of our lives struggling and trying to make things happen one way or another, when the best and brightest things just seem to happen on their own. Isn't that one of the great mantras of just about every sport there is, let the game come to you? Well, it's coming, Jackson, it's coming for you and it's coming for me. In fact, it's never left us.

I used to believe you gotta climb the mountain alone without any help from anyone, but now I see how wrong I was, how believing that can cut you off from everyone you care about and everything that's important. I don't know if I've changed so much as I finally can't avoid the plain hard truth staring me in the face. And I think the same is true for you.

Why not, brother?

Why the hell not?

So things didn't work out the way we planned. So we've fucked up here and there, me more than most. The incredible thing is, there's still some time to make it right — to make *ourselves* right no matter what else life throws our way. I think that's how the grace of God works, letting us fuck everything up on our own so we can finally turn to Him for help. This isn't just your recovering-alcoholic brother talking to you, it's the spirit of a million men and women before me who had to go through the same damn thing and are going through it even now.

I feel real hope for the first time in twenty years, Jackson, and I don't want to blow it. I'm not gonna lose my family over this, and that includes you. We don't have to be heroes anymore, just live a decent life that's involved with other people, people we can try to take care of and help out if we can. That's all it is. So radically simple it makes me wanna laugh and cry out loud at the same time. So maybe my coming out to see you this last time will be a kind of homecoming, the best kind there is. I don't wanna hurt anyone anymore and I don't think you do either when it comes right down to it. I just don't believe it. I *won't* believe it. And I won't let you believe it either.

We need to implement some serious changes. First off is getting you cleaned up and out of that depressing, rundown shack of a house way out there all by yourself. Then we're gonna get you looked at by some doctors, one for your head and one for your body. Doesn't matter what the cost is or how long it takes. We'll take it step by step. I'll be with you all the way. A change of scenery alone would do you a world of good. But if some more radical steps are needed, like putting you somewhere safe and clean where they can take care of you, then we'll do that, too. I don't think you're crazy so much as you need the company and care of other people. You might surprise everyone, Jackson, you might not need help at all. That's a real possibility also.

Someday Scottie will marry and have kids, or maybe he won't. The same with Sam. As long as they're happy, I don't care either way. But we gotta put some of the demons in our blood to rest. We got to find the root of all this pain and anguish and anger and tear it out by the roots before it rises up and explodes in our faces. I'm not a miracle worker, but I think I'm finally coming to realize what we're dealing with here. And I don't just mean his looming shadow. I used to think I had to be father to you in addition to being your older brother because of what he did and what he was, but I've let go of that now. Maybe I should have let you pull the trigger on him the night we saw him drag Mama down the stairs by her hair and you came back into the room with his .45, which was almost bigger than you were.

I just stood there and watched him beat on Mama, but you weren't afraid to stand up to him. You left the room for thirty seconds, then you came back armed at the age of twelve. I know for a fact you would have shot him dead if I hadn't talked you out of it. I don't know what Mama thought, because we never talked about it again. But you had that kind of courage even then, this little scrawny kid wearing an army hat holding a revolver on his own dad. It's almost funny, if it wasn't so damn tragic. I want to hear you laugh, Jackson, I want to see you smile. Jesus, brother, it's been a long time since I've seen you free and easy, just having a good time.

When did we both get so damn serious?

When did everything we do or didn't do become a matter of life and death?

You know what: when I get to Arrowhead maybe we should just go into town to Shooter's and bullshit for a few hours with a cup of black coffee for me and you with whatever you want. I've got some good jokes I haven't sprung on you yet.

I think if I could make you laugh just one more time, really, *really* laugh, a lot of this doom and gloom stuff would just dissolve, evaporate into the atmosphere. Because the truth is, things aren't that bad. They may not be straight-out good, but they're not awful either. If I could just make you see that, Jackson, if my being there could just give you a little bit of light — that would make everything worthwhile. Growing up the way we did we always knew what to do with struggle and setbacks, we just didn't know what to do with being happy. We learned not to trust it somehow. I think that's where we missed the boat: we kept looking in the wrong direction for the things that ailed us or did us harm and the opposite was there all along, or just around the corner. I truly believe that now. No one has to get hurt and no one has to die, least of all yourself.

Just the other day I had lunch with Sam. I met her at a mall outside Glendale. She was a little late getting there so I was sitting by myself when I saw her coming in. She was talking on her cell phone and didn't see me at first — and I'm watching her come toward me, I'm seeing her striding along confidently, her long blond hair sprinkling down around her beautiful face, and I'm thinking, My God, who is this beautiful young woman? Can I really be her father? I swear, Jackson, I was almost intimidated to see my own daughter. When she saw me she broke into a huge smile that lit up the whole place. She waved and my heart just soared, it just about came out of my chest because of a simple thing like that.

Because she meant it and I was there. Because I was gonna have lunch with Sam. Because I was sober and could see things in the clear light of day for once. Because there was real hope in that mall that had nothing to do with me but which still included me somehow. All the hundred, thousand things buzzing all around me that make this world go, no matter how absurd and fucked-up it is. It was enough to go on, to believe in — to think that no matter what we're doing to the ozone layer and whatever the hell else, we're gonna pull through somehow. If I could give you just some small aching sense of that, if you could see it for yourself, the last thing you'd ever think about is hurting anyone or anything. I just don't think you'd have it in you. All that bile and sense of injustice would leak right out of you into the ground.

The way I see it, we're on the verge of turning a momentous corner, Jackson, both of us, you and me: we just need to give each other a little nudge in the right direction. We've reached just about the end of our resources, and that's where God or our guardian angels or whatever else you want to call it can step in and take over. I'm ready to surrender control to a higher power. It's happened enough to me in little ways already for me not to doubt the truthfulness of it. I don't need any other proof.

Let's not be sorry about anything anymore, let's not be so pissed off and raging, trying to figure out where things went wrong in order to make them right. Let's look things in the face and do the best we can with what we got. I know it won't exactly make us world-beaters, but I don't care about that anymore. All that ever did was fuck up my life and take me away from the people I was supposed to take care of. So I'm asking, begging, I'm pleading with you, Jackson, to listen to what I have to say, because I think any other tack you or I try to take will make things worse than they already are. Neither one of us can afford to make that mistake anymore, the one we've been making ever since you almost drowned. You have to meet me halfway. If you do, Jackson, if you really, truly try to, I promise you, little brother, it won't be in vain. Then we can take the next step from there.

Lissa

I asked Ray to leave about twenty minutes ago. When I called and told him Lem had left town he came right over, but that's not why I called him. When he got here I told him I couldn't sleep with him until I told Lem everything. Then he got very quiet, almost somber, but after a little while he said All right, Lissa — you're right: that's only fair.

That's when I knew I love him.

I don't believe in testing people: life itself provides all the tests anyone could ever need. People who say they want to be tested, that they want to be challenged, that they have something to prove to themselves — well, I just don't understand that at all. I'm sorry, I don't. Seems like a sure sign of a lingering adolescence, I don't care how old you are. Because the real tests happen all by themselves without inviting them, and hardly anyone ever passes them with flying colors. It's not that I suddenly sprouted a conscience when it comes to my affair with Ray: no one's that hypocritical. But after a certain point things have to happen in the right order, even if they haven't up till then. I know that's a strange way to rationalize things, but that's how it is.

So here I am waiting for a phone call from Lem, just like I used to do for all those years. But it's different now, I'm different. Only this difference can't be declared just yet. I'm more faithful to him now than I've ever been, even when I was just a girl whose nights consisted of sitting in an empty apartment waiting for him to call me from the road. He'd be gone a month, two months, three — it didn't matter, he could always count on me being right here to pick up the phone on the second or third ring. But someone can only do that for a certain amount of time, I don't care how devoted you are. Eventually something has to give. And it was only much, much later that something did, so much later that it's almost laughable to think of it now, this shell of a marriage that hasn't been a real one for over a decade. We haven't lived under the same roof in seven years, so sometimes I tell myself I'm not being unfaithful at all, because how can you be unfaithful to someone who's never around?

I go over and over it, and you know, it never really does make sense — why we should have drawn it out this long, pretending to be something we haven't been since Sam was still in diapers. The kids don't see us as a couple anyway because ever since they've been alive we've been apart. But that doesn't change the fact that here I am, waiting for Lem to call from somewhere out on the road. He's probably in Colorado by now. That's something I don't know if Lem has ever quite realized: that wherever he goes, he never goes there just by himself. A part of me is always with him, and always will be. I told that to Ray one night after we made love, which wasn't exactly a sensitive thing to say, but Ray didn't take it personally. He understands how complicated it is — or at least he *tries* to understand, which is good enough for me.

It's getting harder and harder for me to say things I don't mean, and Ray catches most of the fallout of this latest development. But he seems to handle it okay. He likes to joke that since we've been together he's developed a thick skin. After Lem gets back and I tell him everything, Ray wants to take me on a trip, I don't even know where. He wants it to be a surprise. I'm really looking forward to that, to just getting away from the shop and everything else. I'm looking forward to it more than I've let on. I don't care where we go. I don't know how Lem will take all of this, but he's had to know somewhere inside that it was a long time coming and, in fact, long overdue: it's not a case of, We can't keep going on like this, but more like, Let's just realize it's been over for a long time now and move on from there. I'm glad he's stopped drinking, but I have to admit I have a wait-and-see attitude: we've been down this road before. Still, this is the longest I've seen him sober, so he seems to have made a real commitment this time. He goes to AA every Wednesday night, sometimes twice, even three times a week, and he's been making a genuine effort with the kids, which is heartbreaking to see.

I don't have the heart to tell him it's too little too late, but apparently they are more resilient and forgiving than I am. They've only known him as this distant and absent figure, so when he's suddenly showing interest in their lives they're a little stunned by his attention. They've learned to have so few expectations of him that when he actually follows through on something, they get a kick out of it, with none of this, *Why weren't you this way before? Where were you all these years?* which I think is a testament to their character. They certainly didn't get it from me. So maybe Lem can even pick up some of the slack as far as parenting goes, which would have been laughable even a year ago. To be honest, I'd enjoy the break, not that they need much from us anymore. I don't worry about my kids that way: they're both responsible, well-adjusted adults with busy, engaged lives of their own. So far I haven't seen any evidence of that Purchase self-destructiveness, so maybe we all dodged a bullet there.

Ray bought an iPod for me and downloaded all these songs he wants me to listen to. But I've only listened to it twice, and not even all the way through. I don't have the heart to tell him how silly I feel putting those things in my ears. So I put it in the sock drawer and try not to think about it. I'm not old-old, but some things are generational, and I like to listen to CDs, which I suppose is more of an advance than Lem, who still listens to his records.

But I don't feel that way about dancing. Ray took me out three nights ago and he was the one who got tired first and had to sit down. I could have danced all night. Once in a while I feel this twinge of recognition — who am I kidding? He's almost eleven years younger than me — but it fades almost as fast as it comes, or maybe I've just learned to suppress it. I'm sure that's it. I told him up front that I'm not interested in starting another family, I've had my kids and went through my thirties and most of my forties and have no desire to relive them. I don't want to relive anything. He said he doesn't want those either and I almost believe him.

I want to believe him, of course. But I've learned enough to know that people's priorities can change, and sometimes overnight. It's true I still look pretty good. I don't know why. I stretch a little and walk every day. I feel as good as I ever have, though I wish I could get rid of a few wrinkles. I smoke three cigarettes a day, tops, but it keeps me from eating more than I should. I don't really care if this is a rationalization or not, I like the peace and stillness a few cigarettes give me. One night not too long ago Sam and I were out having dinner and the guy seated at the table next to us assumed we were sisters and said so, and hey, I'll take that kind of mistaken compliment every time. Sam just rolled her eyes.

Sometimes I worry that I won't be able to keep up with Ray because he's a high-energy, borderline manic person, but on my saner days I just tell myself, So don't keep up. It's not a race. But now it's growing into something very precious and serious to me, almost despite myself. We've even talked about moving in together after the dust settles, if it ever does. I guess if I was more of a bitch than I already am, or more cynical even, more something, I could look at what's happening and say, You got even, Lissa — you got back at Lem for what he put you through all those years: to be with a much younger man who's crazy about you, for Lem to finally wake up out of the life-long fog he's been in and to want to be with you again. But you know, I really don't look at it that way: some things just unfold the way they have to, and it's nobody's single fault and nobody's victory either. I'm not interested in getting back at Lem, or hurting him the way he hurt me. That just seems a total waste of energy and frankly makes me want to cry whenever I think about it.

To suddenly go from basically no man in my life to two all at once is a bit disorienting. Lem always has tended to swing from one extreme to the other, from complete negligence to complete devotion, and I've learned not to trust these swings too much. But it's still curious to me, in an almost detached, objective way, how things are working out, how our lives have evolved to the point they are at now.

The main thing now is Jackson.

I keep telling myself everything's gonna be okay, Lem's finally reached his limit with him, and maybe that's what scares me the most. If Jackson gets a whiff of that — if he somehow comes to realize what Lem is prepared to do — well, I'd rather not think about it, so of course it's all I can think about until he gets back. Jackson senses things about people, like he can read your mind. It's eerie and disturbing. No one can say he's not gifted in his own twisted way, that maybe, maybe at one time it could have been used more positively. But those days are long gone now, and there's no getting them back. If Lem could really understand and accept that one thing it wouldn't be so bad. But for all of his self-destructiveness, Lem is a positive, even optimistic person, especially when it comes to lost causes like Jackson. There's just no putting a dent in his boundless ability to believe in Jackson and give him another chance.

To be honest, it used to make me jealous: I used to think he loved Jackson more than he loved me. And I felt shitty about that, you know, especially after hearing about what they went through growing up and Jackson almost drowning for Lem. It's just one of those situations you can't win: a brother is a brother and a wife is a wife, and no matter what Lem said or tried to say I always knew that Jackson came first, that he was his first priority. All those other fly-by-night women Lem met and slept with on the road over the years didn't affect me as much as his relationship with Jackson, even though he'd sometimes go years not seeing him. I just knew that at the moment of truth or crisis he'd be there for Jackson in a way he never could be there for me. It used to sting and make me bitter until I finally realized there was nothing I could do about it. It's strange how something like jealousy can turn into something else over time, how this fierce and shameful feeling can blossom into sympathy and even acceptance. I'm not jealous of Jackson anymore. I know Lem can't help it, that whatever happened to them happened long before he met me.

I just don't want Lem to get hurt, though it's true, I'm going to hurt him when he comes back. Wherever Lem goes now he's gonna get hurt. I tell myself that the hurt I have for him will eventually be healed and give way to something positive and true — that it will be a temporary hurt that comes out of the truth we've both been avoiding, even apart from the whole situation with Ray. I fully admit this could be another huge rationalization on my part. But Lem's life is in danger when he's around Jackson. I tried to tell him that a hundred times, but he won't listen to me. He says he knows how to handle Jackson, that he's been handling him all his life. But it's the people you're closest to that are the most dangerous. Just ask a battered woman.

One way or another the three of us will always be going back to the day he killed those horses, the three-way secret we haven't shared with anyone else. Scottie or Sam will ask about their uncle once in a while in an offhand way, and every time they do my heart begins to race. I hear these hooves pounding on the ground, I see the dust getting kicked up, I see their teeth big as silver dollars and their wild, cue ball eyes rolling back in their heads. I get frozen with fear, which is exactly what Jackson wants — he wants to produce terror in people. He knows the bible down verse for verse and thinks he's God's right hand or something, which makes him even more dangerous.

Lem's only chance is to stay away from him — and, after this last visit, to have him arrested and sent away. If he won't do it, I will: I'll break my silence and tell the police or the FBI everything Jackson has said and done, everything Lem has told me. I'm prepared to do this even if Lem won't. I went along believing what Lem was saying because I wanted to believe him — that Jackson was getting better, that he had turned a corner, that things were looking up — but that's just not true and never was. I've got all these numbers speed-dialed into my phone, I know exactly who to call and what to say because I've gone over it so many times. Jackson can't be rehabilitated. He can only be sent away and locked up. He has to be stopped before he does something even worse. We're all teetering at an edge and about to fall over into something else, and God help us all when the moment of truth finally arrives, which I know will be different than any of us can imagine, more shocking and more surprising, along with every kind of sorrow that none of us could see coming.

Jackson

See the wild horses on the horizon come out of the early morning mist to slowly become substantial, one then another and another, materializing like canter-bright forms of catastrophic heartbreak. No wild horses around here for a hundred years, but suddenly there they are, beautiful and fierce, as perfect and free as any creature ever was — and you're the one to see them, to cherish and to marvel at their clean lineaments made for vanishing in a headlong thunder of sound. It's like you're born again in just seeing them, in knowing they are there at the first light of dawn. You try to choke back the sobs geysering in your throat but they break out and flood your face anyway, and this weeping pries you open like a bride for the Lord to enter in a single cry of Oh sweet dear God.

For your brother, for the one who loves you. For the way he holds a cigarette after his life has fallen apart and he sits there in the ashes. For the mother who gave you life. For the father who tried to take it away. For your God, your country, for the ones who have to die before the setting of the sun. For the ones who have never truly lived. For the fucking love of it all and the waste that blew you out of the void to hurl you straight back into it. I can't put it any other way, Lissa: the mercy makes me speak it so. Then the heart-stopping horses, horses never brushed or saddled by human hand with the light pouring out of them, sparks buried in their manes:

How would you stroke and stoke them, breathing them into fire?

They didn't come all this way to be denied and awed over, they came to be bequeathed. I knew it like the rain. So I couldn't not see them for what they were. I couldn't sit there and pretend the Lord hadn't answered all my prayers. Because suddenly there they were. It was I who'd been the doubting one. I knew they were Lem's horses even if he couldn't know or accept it, even if no one did, including you: nothing could change the fact that they were his and had always been his.

I didn't want to kill them but they kept getting closer, beckoning me. They were curious about dying on the cross, you see. They saw the world in my tears and the unfettered lands they used to roam, which kept shrinking by the day. They saw me come out of the house with the rifle in one hand and the bible in the other and a rucksack on my back. They saw I was a broken son and lost brother. They saw I was a ragged piece of pale flesh hanging on the crucified hand of God. So they kept getting closer, getting nearer, the roan with the diamond on its forehead leading the way, its shot-glass nostrils flaring like the blowhole of a whale, gaining in size and majesty, rising up out of the continent and American history, swamping out the rest of my life in a moan.

God gave me a vision through these horses, and this is what I saw: I saw Union and Confederate soldiers staggering between them with their arms falling off from gangrene. I saw punch-drunk Vietnam vets with blood pouring out of their ears and F-14s screaming without sound a mere hundred feet above the ground. I saw headlines ten stories high, chronicling the mayhem and madness of our age, barking giant black block letters in an ether of threadbare sky. Abe kept getting blasted in the back of the head, Kennedy's head snapped back like a crash-test dummy, his eyes big as eggs. I saw the plains open and swallow the highways, I saw a mushroom cloud off in the distance with the billowing forehead of yon withered patriarch. Joe Louis was fucking a white woman, Elvis caught the blue wave of his own electric hair. Lem was a high-light reel, chasing down balls hit hard in the gap or out near the warning track, crashing into the wall again and again and again but holding onto the ball. The top ten plays on ESPN made up of a single player.

To see through horses you have to be broken and lost and raised on distance, you have to know that your own pitiful life has some purpose and redemption value, even if no one else can see it: that you are made for a promise whose fulfillment is close at hand. You must be a reject with an outcast's sense of loneliness and exile even within your own hometown, treated like a smudge of shit on the back of someone's boot heel.

I've always believed that a light comes pouring up out of the bodies of recently killed animals and people, a light that no one on earth can see with the naked eye, that goes back all the way to the stars. I believe that dying isn't the final word but the very first word, that what death says is more important in its silence than any bird that deigns to sing on its swaying branch in a tree. Truth was, I wanted to warn those horses, tell them that they should run away, but there was no way I could rightly deny what they were offering me, which was offering itself.

One horse rippled with stars like the flag on a pole above a schoolyard, stars announcing the chosen and beloved of God and the very breath he breathes along with a wilderness of downed power lines and trees after a storm. The others fanned out behind him, trotting with heads held high, their barrel chests shimmering like curtains of northern lights. They were coming closer, getting nearer to the house, because I was the one who would lead them to the glory of their deaths. I stood there with mouth agape, trying to mumble out words of warning and praise.

I don't want to kill your horses,

I told Lem when we were kids, and he looked at me like I'd had a bad dream. What are you talking about, Jackson? When did I ever even ride a horse? I said, But they're yours, Lem—you just don't know it yet. I tried to tell him. I got all emotional, but he couldn't hear me for what I was trying to tell him. It's not his fault. The words just came years in front of their arrival forty years later, is all. He didn't know they were his.

I was righteous before I knew it, I was God's faulty instrument that hadn't yet been broken enough in order to receive his call. It's not about me or what I have to do: it's not us and misunderstanding charging the air between us. I try to tell it like it is but it comes out all confused. I know how crazy it sounds. But I knew about those horses before they got there, I knew that they were Lem's. I knew that I loved them enough to kill them and that blood is just the last criterion of a sacrifice that will flower in the dust.

I know I'm disturbed, Lissa, but there's a truth in the disturbance, like a seismic tremor quaking inside the ground. You wouldn't say the earth is crazy, would you—the monsoon rains, the hurricanes, the—God forbid—acts of God that rain down devastation by water, wind, and fire? Just look around. You'll see madness itself showing up everywhere, only everyone calls it normal and the status quo. I'm talking television, billboards galore, phones so small they can plant them in your ears, everywhere where people live a constant noise. It wasn't always like that, and the horses showed me that. They had come to me for their deaths. They had come to *me*, Lissa, no one else. How could I deny them what they had come for, wandering all over the west, trying to kick in the heads of

84

cougars? If they could no longer be wild and free, they couldn't go on living. I wanted them to live for what they were made for, and, if they couldn't, why then, to go down with some kind of dignity at the hands of someone who understood.

So I couldn't unsummon what had finally found me. I couldn't say to my Father in heaven: I no longer accept the gifts you are giving me after I've been asking for them all this time. Lem's horses had turned me into their beacon, and *Why me Lord?* I already knew the answer. I had died once and could show them how it was done. I could prepare the way. Dying is a precious art form, the one this country has dismissed and tried to get away from. But if you do not die, then you cannot live the way you were meant to live. I can't put it any other way, there's no other way to say it.

I stepped off the porch and started walking toward them, speaking softly as I went. They bolted in all directions, just as I knew they would, but they didn't go far. They came back to the invisible center where everything was one and I walked on the outside rim of that holy perimeter. I can tell you what I told them, but it will only make sense if you're able to see the birth and death of nations in the bodies of wild horses.

I know why you came here,

I said: I know what it means to you. I've always known.

They smelled something in it, something like honey with a voice dripping inside it. My voice. I didn't have to make promises, I was their stone-cold fulfillment.

Come out with me to a place I know, a place that God has made ready for you. You'll find apples and sugar cubes there, and clean, waving grasses as high as your knees. You don't have to be afraid.

I walked ahead and didn't look back, speaking just loud enough for them to hear me, and they followed. I bent down and picked a wildflower and put it between my teeth, and it tasted like the poor simple truth that only beggars know. We were taking a journey together, but it wouldn't be very far. I knew where I had to lead them, I knew where we had to go, out near the old Sanderson place that's been abandoned for twenty years. There was something about my voice that even I could hear, its cracking husks and tones, and I heard it with their ears. I told them what was happening and what was going to happen. I didn't demean them with a half-hearted lie. I know they understand. They followed me like the clouds and far-off explosions they were destined to become. I had a bullet for each one of them, but that wouldn't be near enough. I could already see their legs kicking up in the air when I came in with the knife.

You see how God works, don't you — you see how it's not about comfort or convenience or letting others do the dirty work for you. You have to do it yourself. Don't mean a shit that you don't wanna be a part of it or have no taste for blood. If you don't, you become a lie unto yourself, blooming out in false particulars. You're participating in a falsehood, an evasion, like everyday pornography and desecration. You're an outright fucking whore. This is why the Romans had to tear off His clothes and drive in the nails, why they spat on Him and drew out the agony. He meant to show us something by going through what He did. He didn't allow others to do his dying for Him. He didn't stand back and say, *Now you go take care of it.* He let Himself be swallowed up in the blood and the shit and the tears, and He came out victorious. But only after He was fucking tortured, ridiculed, and killed. So there are no Christs left in America, unless they're sleeping in homeless shelters. We're too entertainable and overweight for that. The rest of us are out-and-out Romans, every last one. But even a Roman has to do what he is called to do: take up his appointed spear and stick it in God's side.

There's an art to killing horses, they don't just bunch together where you can shoot them and they die for you. You've got to orchestrate it with care. Once they followed me out the four miles to the Sanderson place I had to get them to go the final distance, only about thirty feet. I stopped at the gate, took out some rope, and tied it to the swinging latch and told them this was also part of it, toward the very end. They trusted my voice, but the rest of me they weren't so sure about. I walked into the enclosure with fencing seven feet high and they stayed back near the entrance, just standing there. The white one even stamped its forelegs into the ground, like a kind of half-hearted protest. I turned my back on them, dropped to my knees and closed my eyes with that rope in my hand. I'd coax them to come in by being a proper disciple, I'd be the last and only holy man they saw in their light golden dreams of falling hay. But it wasn't just for them: I dropped because that was the only thing I could do then, the only thing I could be. The name Abraham ran through my head like a hymn playing the same refrain over and over.

I don't know how long I stayed there on my knees, but it felt like forever. The sun pressed up against my eyelids and I saw angels made of sunspots. After a long time I heard them come in one by one behind me, the most beautiful and delicate sound I ever heard, like they had grown spider legs and were stepping into a land covered with daffodils and question marks. Nobody ever loved the ground they walked on more. One of them growled deep inside its throat, another one seemed to almost whine. The snort, the blow, the nicker, the neigh, the squeal leading up to the scream. They were trying to ask me something, but I couldn't answer them in words. I felt no guilt at the prospect of what I had to do, only a terrible resolve.

When they were all in I asked the Lord one last time to be relieved of what He had asked, but I already knew the answer. I've always known the answer. I flung myself forward as hard as I could and heard the latch shut home, the snake of the rope springing up between them like the tail of a startled cat. I scrambled my way to the closest fence ten feet away and got kicked in the right hand. It went so numb it was like it belonged to somebody else. Then I clambered up the fence out of the way of their charging hooves. They were churning the dust all around in a funnel cloud as I sat on the top of the fence, watching them. I think a few of them wished they had hands and arms to climb after me and tear me to shreds. My hand began to throb, but I couldn't take my eyes away from the swirling storm before me.

Then I carried out what I was called to do, the prophecy manifest in my veins. None of them died right away. One shot wasn't enough for any of Lem's horses. They grew so intimate with the ground it was like they were being born out of it, snapping teethward to the sun. I was their way out and upward, even as they were mine. We had a connection in a way no one could deny. To walk between dying horses is to feel yourself almost soaring, with your shadow moving over them in a towering sundial. The whole world was inside each one of their crazed eyeballs, but I didn't look away. I watched them as I knelt down and slit their throats, and they watched me. Now you know it for yourself, Lissa: I killed Lem's horses, and I did not begrudge the duty of it, because it cleared the path for what had to be done, which is not anything anyone can stop because it's almost here.

RECKONING

The dark blue '94 Century comes west down the gravel road four miles outside of Arrowhead, Nebraska, a sere, cumulus cloud of dust rising two stories high before it disintegrates in the bright empty air where the horizon runs out and drops away into the gaping mouth of the sky. Only the Century moves across the hard scrabble tabletop of earth at forty miles an hour, the rhythmic clicking and rumble of gravel and small stones constant as rain and cast out like spent rounds after making their brief loop-de-loops in the wheel wells, the driver ram-rod straight with both hands on the wheel and dark marauder sunglasses to match the lunar inscape of his imminent arrival to a place held at the taut shrieking tension of violin strings.

Inside the car the lonesome, yodeling voice of Hank Williams can be heard going down in heartbreak with no relief in sight, the driver motionless and almost frozen, a statue driver or dummy in life-sized reprieve doing its utmost to keep the car in the middle of the road, which tapers off at each side like a continuous and overturned canoe. Radiating out in every direction is the vast, empty bell tone of a nothingness so unremitting it once drove pioneers to madness, clawing their way out of covered wagons to run out into the fields and shoot themselves in the head or explode Godward into babble. Some naïf or otherworldly traveler might wonder what keeps the Century from floating off into outer space, but the car remains affixed to its headlong trajectory, its stone driver perfectly intact.

Five miles away the gravel road breaks into an intersection heading north and south. Three hundred yards beyond stands a tiny, single-level clapboard house the color of faded eggshell, with one of its shutters hanging like a picture frame about to swing free and a step-up porch the size of a dumbwaiter. One of its two windows is covered with plastic sheeting whose frayed and ghostly edges lifts its skirt every time the wind kicks up. The house is off in fields of long waving grass like a house lost at sea with no discernible yard to speak of, unless that yard entailed the whole continent. A powder blue Chevy pickup stands off to the side of the house with a bulging tarp-covered load tied down expertly with leather straps. Next to it is a white septic tank with a rusting underbelly like a one-man submarine heaped up upon the plains. The house has no borders, no markers, no signs whatsoever that it has ever had visitors, let alone the extravagance of a single neighbor.

Jutting out from the unsheeted window is a 24-inch fluted sniper barrel aiming at the intersection where the Century is headed. From the road you cannot see the barrel unless you have been trained to look for it, so shutter-dark and asshole small it looks like a spec of nil surrounded by the brighter and blowing void. The barrel does not move nor so much as waver half a degree up or down, but lays an even five feet above the ground for the shot that will shatter the plains' equipoise into thunder. The cloud of dust raised by the Century is visible from the house like an oncoming token of foreboding, the only thing that gives the horizon a glimpse of fleeting change.

From inside the house a calm, deadpan voice begins to recite Chapter 6 from the Book of Revelation in a steady tone that does not belie the strangeness of its content: "Now I saw when the Lamb opened one of the seven seals, and I heard one of the four living creatures say, as with a voice of thunder, 'Come!' And I saw, and behold, a white horse, and its rider had a bow; and a crown was given to him, and he went out conquering and to conquer. When he opened the second seal, I heard the second living creature say, 'Come!' And out came another horse, bright red; its rider was permitted to take peace from the earth, so that men should slay one another; and he was given a great sword. When he opened the third seal, I heard the third living creature say 'Come!' And I saw, and behold, a black horse, and its rider had a balance in his hand; and I heard what seemed to be a voice in the midst of the four living creatures saying, 'A quart of wheat for a denarius, and three quarts of barley for a denarius, but do not harm oil and wine!' When he opened the fourth seal, I heard the voice of the fourth living creature say, 'Come!' And I saw, and behold, a pale horse, and its rider's name was Death, and Hades followed him; and they were given power over a fourth of the earth, to kill with sword and with famine and with pestilence and by wild beasts of the earth." Before long the Century materializes out of the cloud of dust, scarab-blue and gaining. The voice inside the house continues reciting Revelation, growing just slightly louder with every word as the bolt action of the rifle clicks into well-oiled place like the bright brass latch of a door. The voice hovers above the ground as the Century comes within half a mile of the intersection. "Then the kings of the earth and the great men and the generals and the rich and the strong, and every one, slave and free, hid in the caves and among the rocks of the mountains, calling to the mountains and the rocks, "Fall on us and hide us from the face of him who is seated on the throne, and from the wrath of the Lamb; for the great day of his wrath has come, and who can stand before it?" The first shot rips the front right tire completely off the Century as if it had been detonated from the axis to launch perpendicular and northward of the moving car: the Century veers sharply off to the right and barrels

93

out into the fields with the giant lash of a dust cloud curving around to follow it before the car comes to a sliding halt. The second shot shatters the driver's left clavicle and spins him around as he is getting out of the car to end up in a heap on the ground. A single eyelash wisp of gunsmoke comes briefly out of the rifle's barrel before both it and the barrel disappears, retreating back like a needle being drawn out of still water. Then the house and the land it's on and the road go back to their immense and unbroken sorrow, with just a puff of breeze to caress them. The driver is croaking and whimpering on the ground, saying Jesus, Jesus, over and over again, but he cannot be readily seen from the house. The shooter detaches the scope from the m24 and pans the scene where he has fired two shots sixteen seconds apart. When he finally sees the driver half-rocking and rolling on the ground he puts down the scope and walks out the door, calmly adding another round to the chamber as he goes.

Lem

Jesus, Jesus, Jackson — you shot me?

You actually fucking shot me?

Lissa

If I could do it over again, if I had just one more chance, five minutes, forty seconds, I would have told Lem everything before he left this last time, I would have laid it all out on the table with nothing left to spare. Complete and total disclosure: maybe then he would have been too broken and devastated to leave, to care what Jackson's latest issue or darkly veiled plan is.

I hate it that Lem can still do this to me, even though I know he doesn't do it on purpose, which makes me hate it even more. I hate Lem and I hate myself, especially myself for allowing this to happen again. And if Ray tries to call after I told him not to even think about it, I'll hate him, too.

But most of all I hate Jackson for putting us through this again, for dredging up the past and some imagined future where he dangles us like puppets. I hate him for his twisted heart and I hate him because he was willing to drown for Lem when they were kids. I hate him that he's crazy, that he can't tell a lie. I wish he were dead and incinerated from the earth forever. All I can do now is imagine the worst, and the worst with Jackson is pretty damn grim. I can't eat, I can't sleep, I'm within arm's length of the phone at all times.

All my so-called grains of possibility and hardwon empowerment have officially flown right out the window. I'm just quaking little Melissa Purchase again, pacing around in her bathrobe and shuffling across the kitchen floor, waiting for the phone to ring. It's like the clock's been turned back twenty years. I don't want anyone to see me like this, so now I'm a shut-in. If Ray tries to call and ask me how I am I'll be very pissed off but also grateful, I'll break down crying and shout into the phone. The only person I want to hear from at this point is Lem.

Twenty-four hours, that's what I'm giving him — and if I don't hear from Lem I'm calling the state police and opening the floodgates. I'll tell them everything. I'll tell them what Jackson did to those horses and all the other things he's hinted at over the years. I'll tell them about the barns he blew up, the things Lem has alluded to without outright saying them. I'll make it sound like a national emergency because that's exactly what it is. I'm not fucking around anymore: if Lem doesn't call and tell me he's okay in two more hours, I'll make sure Jackson never sees the light of day again. To Jackson I may only be Lem's cheating, estranged wife, but if he does anything to my husband, the man I'm currently married to and have been for twenty-five years, I'll make him pay for the rest of his lfie.

All my life I've had these pathetic, delayed reactions to things, drawn-out responses that come up long after the actual event. But that's starting to change. I'm starting to get pissed off now and it's simmering up to the surface. I've had it with the Purchase brothers, with the Purchase name and all that it entails, the weeping guitars playing in every corner. My slippers keep whispering that something is slipping away as they brush across the linoleum floor. I can't help what they're saying. This is the absolute last time, I can't do it anymore. I must have been crazy to agree to it in the first place.

Go ahead and drive out to Nebraska, Lem, it's got nothing to do with me anymore. Get yourself blown up with your insane brother. I can't believe we let it go this far. We're both delusional for not seeing this for what it is, for allowing Jackson to get away with the last five years. He's cast a spell over you, over me, over our entire lives, a dark cloud following us everywhere we go. I don't want to hear about mitigating circumstances, how he drowned for you, how you had to practically raise him. None of that has the power to move me anymore. The whole pathetic psychodrama has sucked me dry.

Just call and tell me you're okay. Just come back in one piece. Please, Lem. That's all I'm asking of you. If you don't, I'll hurt you myself. But I would never hurt you, would I, Lem? I can't even joke about it. Tell me where you are. Tell me it's okay, just like you used to. Jackson would never hurt you, just like you said. You admitted this, you convinced yourself and me that this was the case, a self-fulfilling prophecy. So make it come true, Lem. Please, baby. Just this one last time. You're okay. You're safe. Just one last false alarm. Breathe it into the phone, tell it to me in your road-weary voice. You're safe, you're fine, everything's okay. I'm waiting to hear from you, Lem. I'm right here. So just call and say it, okay? Then we can talk. Then we can say it and trust it and believe it. I'm waiting for you, the kids are waiting for you. The whole country. All you have to do is call. Then we can go from there. Please, Lem. Please.

REVELATION

The one who's shot crabs and crawls his way under the car, trailing a swath of blood. The shooter calls out in a loud, clear voice: I'm sorry it had to be this way, brother. I only shot you because I had to. You don't have to feel bad about me drowning for you. Now you can drown for me. *The wounded man drags himself between the two front tires with his shattered shoulder dangling like a broken trap. He stares at the shooter's boots coming across the gravel road less than a quarter of a mile away. They look familiar somehow, like he's seen them somewhere before, maybe even worn them in the souped-up clarity of a dream. The taste of aluminum closes around his tongue like an iron cage.* Only the Lord can stop the bleeding now. But I love you, brother, you're the only family I ever really had. *The wounded man bows his head in the direction of the approaching figure and groans. He starts to vomit up a sob, but it subsides just as fast. He wants to cry out to the one who shot him, but his mouth is drier than sand.*

Instead he starts shimmying backward with his good elbow as a stumping cane, his wild eyes rooted to the oncoming boots before they disappear from view. Then he crawls into the tall, waving grass,

*parting its shimmering loom with a startled yelp every few inches to
punctuate the shock of agony and betrayal. The shooter keeps walking at his deliberate pace in the direction of the car, talking about
sacrifice and the power of redemption. The wounded man thinks,*
At least he didn't break the windshield, *but doesn't know why he
thinks it at such a time. He wants to believe if he crawls far enough
into the long grass then maybe he can wait to die on his back, staring
up at the sky. Or figure out why his brother shot him. Or somehow
be raised to the brink of an overwhelming light. Or sink even further
down into pain. Or wait for anyone but the shooter to find him.
Or wait. Yes, just that. Just wait.* I keep seeing the kingdom, Lem.
I've seen it ever since I drowned, like a moth to the candlelight.
It's calling me out, it's calling you out, calling everyone out. That's
how the kingdom works. I'm taking my pickup to the state capitol
building and I'm not coming back. It's strictly one way. So when
the Sower comes toppling down from his tower in the sky they'll
finally understand. But first they have to feel the shock and the
terror. Because that's the way it's got to be. *The wounded man hears
the shooter as a far-off, calling bell tolling ever closer, coming his
way like a looming chime. He wants to believe he can crawl away
at the pace of ten feet an hour, that the grass can hide and protect
him, maybe even turn him into one of their sawing and soughing
own. It would be nice to be a tall stem of waving grass like all the
others but different, too. You could hide right out in the open then.
Grass is a beautiful thought when you're about to die, good enough
practically for see-through. There's no reason he can't become the
size of a snail, a worm, a mica fleck of deep dark loam; no reason
he can't hide himself away in all the brooming lushness that seems
to go on forever. No reason at all.* They'll build monuments to you,
Lem, they'll call you a hero. Because you're the one who tried to
reach me, tried to make me see the light. I'm telling it this way to
make you understand. You're dying just a few hours before I'll die

myself. I didn't shoot you to hurt you, I shot you to save you and make you immortal. You're almost there, brother, almost there. *The shooter stops suddenly, yelling out,* BROTHER! I LOVE YOU! FORGIVE ME! *But the wounded man doesn't pay him any mind. He's focusing instead on getting smaller and disappearing, getting so neat and tidy he can fit in the palm of a little girl's hand; he's concentrating on the ground before him that appears so clear and charged it's like he's some intimate explorer of a new world. He doesn't think about dying anymore. Instead he wonders at size, at moles, at the eyelash legs of certain spiders walking over a melon. His son's face is a halo, his daughter's laughter the voice of an angel. Facts are something you can work with, mold into miracles. Lissa's blue eyes hold all the water I ever want to swim in. Maybe Jackson's right to be God-haunted: he's goddamn everywhere, brighter than rain or honey, touching the grass with fingers made of sunlight. Here I find out I'm a halleluiah — whoever would have thought of that, he says two seconds before he crawls a few more feet, bows his head, and passes out.*

How do they come?

How do they manage to take over the earth?

The shooter cannot hear it, but he feels it trembling up through his boot soles, so gradual at first he confuses it with his own sudden and abject wailing. He stops and wipes the tears from his face. He bends to the ground like he's about to kiss it, a pilgrim arriving at a holy place after traveling for years, the faint vibrations filling up his body.

Is it an unrailed train approaching, an earthquake, a charging and invading army? The earth is coming alive, trembling unto itself like an eager child. He's an instrument, a lover, a medium through which the air and ground met for the first time and exchange electromagnetic waves. The wounded man is dark dank in the grass, slowly leaking out of himself. He has no consciousness left to countenance it. The shooter is face-down on the ground with his limbs extended, a man caught in radical free fall on his way to the center of the earth. He could be a da Vinci drawing, a chalk outline of someone killed in a drive-by shooting. Both men are draped across the ground like rag dolls, even as the earth gives back a tremor so faint it's like the outermost breath-beat of someone about to sneeze or on the verge of an orgasm, of coming itself. The horizon's an arrow and something is drawing it back, getting it poised and ready for flight. The shooter cries out LEM? LEM? but the wounded man does not answer.

He feels them before he hears them, kicking up a continent of dust filled with the changing wine light of the setting sun, fata morganas of rolling cycloramas and epic battles played out across the sky: Nagasaki and Hiroshima with rolls of shock waves rippling out ten miles wide and every Fourth of July fireworks display, volcanoes erupting tons of ash spewing out into the atmosphere, blitzkriegs and meteorites striking the earth, and the death of every star.

The shooter doesn't look up.

He doesn't want to see, doesn't want to give it its due. He lies facedown and still under the changing, charging hues of the sky, feeling them come on while the wounded one sleeps on in his half mud mask of dirt and blood. Before long the ground seems to almost

jump against the shooter's reverent cheek, commanding him to, Look,
see for yourself, *but still he keeps his eyes closed. It's only after he
thinks they're almost on top of him that he finally lifts his head and
slowly opens his eyes.*

*Clouds of dust rising ever higher take on the churning, changing
shapes of Mt. Rushmore and the Shroud of Turin, weeping grand-
mothers in headscarves, Ferris wheels at Disneyland: he sees the
Taj Mahal and Chartes Cathedral, the World Trade Center going
down and the madcap heads of woodpeckers. He sees battleships in
the South Pacific and Ford assembly lines working double overtime,
dogs being sicked on Negroes in the 1950s in Birmingham in grainy
newsreels. He sees all fifty United States and their respective license
plates swaying like wind chimes in a breeze, he sees the face of MLK
and his pencil mustache perspiring truth and justice. He sees writh-
ing orgies and cocksuckers galore before they turn into windswept
dunes covering up corporate crimes and John Wayne leaning and
tipping his hat in a doorway.*

*He slowly gets to his feet and watches them come — and before
long he can make out a stampede of wild horses coming straight for
him over the horizon, horses nobody has ever seen before the size of
giant earthmovers, the sky suddenly becoming the color of crushed
grapefruit with streaks of white-out shooting tracers in the seams. The
shooter doesn't move. From a distance the manes of the wild horses
look like dancing spiders before they become bigger than flocks of
white birds and then a prairie fire raging out of control. He drops his
rifle and stretches out his arms, like a human scarecrow. The ground
no longer trembles but rumbles and shakes as if the continental plates
are about to break through the integument of the earth. He closes
his eyes to the tidal wave of oncoming horses moments before they
arrive; he vanishes instantly when they rush over him, as if he had
never been.*

A hoof the size of a Volkswagon steps down on the roof of the Chevy

truck by the house and compacts it straight into the ground, deto-
nating almost instantaneously the tight-fitting load and its megaton
contents that blow the house away like it's made of pickup sticks in
a sudden furnace blast of inferno. The horses' eyes are bigger than
mansion windows, crazed and headlong staring, their door-sized
teeth snapping shut and flying open again. One of them stops and
rears up to the height of a five-storey building, rabbit punching the
air in swaths of dark threatening clouds that become double-barreled
tornados twisting their way back to earth in the form of giant striking
cobras. Hail the size of grapefruit starts to pour down and everything
is a swirl of wind and rain. The plunging, lunging jaws of horses big
as motorboats with lightning bolts lighting up sheets of place as the
horses merge and run through each other, no way to tell where the
earth begins and the air ends.

The wounded man suddenly comes to in a moan inside the eye of
the swirling tumult all around him; he raises his head half an inch to
see with sudden and hallucinatory clarity an Amish family fourteen
strong floating by at their own solemn pace, upright in a wagon, levi-
tating around like dark holy satellites untouched by the swirling wind
and debris, devout members of the same Mennonite sect, somberly
dressed, riding in their starched collars, the women with bonnets on
their heads and the men with hats, looking straight ahead as becomes
their quiet dignity, humming a gospel tune, the stark wooden patri-
arch leading them with stone eyeballs and a buggy whip across his
knees, the men's beards tracing their granite jaws with no mustaches
to speak of, all of them beclouded within the charging clouds in a
sepia haze or afterglow, at peace in the stampeding storm, not of this
world, with a little girl pulling up the rear, shaking a tambourine made
of a copperhead's rattle that never warned anyone from its hidden
copse of stones. He sees a chimpanzee riding and bucking the gable
of a house before it and the gable are sucked into the black pit of a
vortex whisked away forever, pieces from a John Deere museum and

a dead man driving a Studebaker with his mouth full of sand. He collapses his cheek again and closes his eyes, conscious but unwilling to see anything more.

The charging tornado horses are everywhere and they do not abate, do not give the wounded man any chance to shake his head and clear it of what he had just seen. So he lies there and hugs the grass that holds him, which is enough because it's all he has. He's hurt bad but he's not dead, and then suddenly, almost abruptly, the tornados in the form of horses or horses in the form of tornados lift and disappear. He's afraid to open his eyes, he doesn't trust them. The barometric pressure drops and fluctuates, then stabilizes. He's sure, he's positive he's dead.

But he isn't. After fifteen minutes, after twenty or an hour, he slowly tries to push up on his good side. The pain jangles through him so he falls back down and almost passes out again. After three more rickety tries he finally gets to his feet and reels around like a drunk before he gains some kind of balance. Then he knows what he has always somehow known and somehow forgotten, who and what he was always meant to be: a man staggering and walking out of a field at twilight, trying to find his way home.

Cold Snap as Yearning, University of Nebraska Press (2001)
The Mover of Bones, University of Nebraska Press (2006)
Lamb Bright Saviors, Unviersity of Nebraska Press (2010)

To order or obtain more information on these or other University of Nebraska Press titles, visit www.nebraskapress.unl.edu.

Breinigsville, PA USA
13 January 2011
253221BV00003B/1/P